FRIENDS OR FOES?

"Shana," Katie said, "you didn't know Mitch was going to dump you when you started out. How could you have known that?"

Shana shrugged. "I don't know. Do you think I just didn't . . . you know, turn him on?"

"Oh, Shana!" Katie said. "You're so gorgeous, how can you think that?"

"Well then, what went wrong?"

"I don't know. He's a funny guy. . . ." Katie's voice trailed off.

Why is Katie defending Mitch? Shana wondered. Even though she played opposite Mitch on the show, Katie claimed they didn't get along. Or did they. . . .? If they didn't get along, then how come Katie knew more about him than his own girlfriend?

Other series from Bantam Books for Young Readers
Ask your bookseller for the books you have missed.

ALL THAT GLITTERS #2

TAKE TWO

Kristi Andrews

BANTAM BOOKS
TORONTO · NEW YORK · LONDON · SYDNEY · AUCKLAND

RL 6, IL age 12 and up

TAKE TWO
A Bantam Book / November 1987

ISBN 0-553-26417-6

Published simultaneously in the United States and Canada

Bantam Books are published by Bantam Books, Inc. Its trade-
mark, consisting of the words "Bantam Books" and the por-
trayal of a rooster, is Registered in U.S. Patent and Trademark
Office and in other countries. Marca Registrada. Bantam
Books, Inc., 666 Fifth Avenue, New York, New York 10103.

PRINTED IN THE UNITED STATES OF AMERICA

O   0 9 8 7 6 5 4 3 2 1

Take Two

★

One

Shana Bradbury usually enjoyed going to work. She had been a regular on "All That Glitters," the sizzling top-rated soap opera, for almost a year. But that morning was different. That day her grandmother, Edith Bradbury, was to join the "All That Glitters" cast.

Edith's arrival would be wonderful for the show, of course; Edith was one of the most popular performers on daytime TV. But for Shana it was bad news. Although Edith rarely interfered with Shana's personal life, she kept an eagle eye on her granddaughter's career. Shana was sure her acting would suffer with Edith breathing down her neck every minute.

"Shana! Please pay attention to me when I am talking to you."

Reluctantly, Shana swiveled her head toward her grandmother. The limousine they were riding in was only minutes from the soap's studio on Manhattan's West Side. Edith was tense. She was like a firecracker ready to explode.

"Sorry—were you saying something to me?" Shana asked.

Edith's blue eyes flashed dangerously. "You know perfectly well I was. I was telling you about today's schedule. Now, pay attention. And sit up straight too. You are a human being, not a piece of spaghetti."

Shana pulled herself up. She didn't like being ordered around, but when Edith used her marine drill sergeant voice she had no choice but to obey. Even a stone would jump.

"Now, where was I?" Edith asked herself, patting her white hair to be sure it was all in place. "Oh, yes—our arrival. It should be quite spectacular. My fans will be on hand to welcome me to 'All That Glitters.' The press will be there too. Please be prepared to answer their questions."

"Yes, Grandma."

"Next, I will be meeting with the producer. It's a private meeting, but afterward I want you to be around. I may have an announcement."

"Uh-huh."

Edith turned, studying her. "You know, it wouldn't hurt you to show a little more enthusiasm, Shana. This is a big day for me. In fact, it is a big day for both of us."

Shana just shrugged.

"Shana, is there something wrong?" her grandmother demanded.

"No, nothing's wrong." What good would it do to explain my feelings? Shana wondered. Edith wouldn't understand.

"Are you sure?" Edith persisted.

"Sure, I'm sure! I'm just tired, all right? Seven-fifteen A.M. is not my favorite time of day."

"I've noticed," Edith said dryly. "Still, getting up early is part of being a soap actress, Shana. If you don't like it, then maybe you should go into another line of work."

Shana wondered if her grandmother had any idea how often she fantasized about doing just that. At times it seemed to her that anything, anything at *all*, would be better than acting.

She stared out the limo's tinted window at Central Park. It wasn't that she didn't enjoy acting, she reminded herself—she did. The problem was that, thanks to Edith, she had been performing for twelve of her seventeen years. She was tired of it. She wanted a break—a chance to stop pretending to be other people all the time and start being herself.

The limousine rolled on. Outside, it was a typical New York summer morning: hazy, hot, and humid. Early-morning joggers crowded the roadside, their T-shirts as brightly colored as confetti.

Shana slipped into a daydream, picturing what it would be like to be an ordinary seventeen-year-old. No lines to learn, no twelve-hour days to struggle through, no pressure. On a day like today she'd go shopping. Or maybe hit the beach. Whatever it was, it would be relaxing—and light-years away from the "Glitters" studio and Edith.

Edith. Her daydream dissolved as she thought about her grandmother. She had lived with Edith since she was two, yet in all that time she had never gotten used to her grandmother's tyrannical ways. Why was it that whenever her grandmother barked an order—or told her about a new role she wanted her to audition for—she was seized by an angry panic? Reacting that way never did any good.

Maybe I take after my mother, she thought. She barely knew her mother, Barbara Bradbury. But she had read about her often. Episodes from her mother's stormy life were plastered across the supermarket tabloids almost any week. Anything from her mother's angry rejection of her Hollywood career, to her marriage to Shana's father (an Arab prince), to her messy divorce from the prince when Shana was two, to the dozens of comeback attempts her mother always ruined with booze.

At least Mom got away, she thought. I'm stuck with Edith, and whenever I fight with her, I lose. It was utterly depressing.

Suddenly the limo's partition slid back. "We'll be arriving at the studio shortly," the driver announced.

Quickly Shana checked herself in the window's reflection. I look okay, she decided. Her thick dark brown hair was tamed in a braid, and her olive-toned skin was subtly highlighted with makeup. She'd pass. Too bad she couldn't say the same for her dress. It was one her grandmother had picked out, and she hated it. With its virginal white collar and dainty half sleeves, it made her feel like Miss Priss.

Edith glanced over. "You look very nice today, Shana. Very professional."

"Thanks," Shana mumbled. "You look pretty good too."

That, at least, was true. Edith had done herself up wonderfully for her arrival at the studio. She wore a striking green silk sheath dress and a rope of huge pearls. Not that she needed elegant clothes; her distinguished face and magnetic presence always assured her of instant recognition.

As the limo left Central Park and began sliding up the West Side, the tension in the car grew stronger. Shana was nervous. She didn't like appearing before huge crowds. And that morning was going to be especially difficult since the crowd would all be Edith's adoring fans. Would they even notice Shana as they cheered for her grandmother, the Queen of the Soaps?

A moment later the limo turned the final corner and came to a stop in front of the studio. As it did, Shana stared out the window in disbelief.

"Drat!" Edith hissed. "I was afraid this would happen."

As expected, a crowd had gathered, but it was not on hand to welcome Edith. On the contrary, the fans were there to protest her departure from "Destiny's Children," the soap she had starred in before her switch to "All That Glitters." They were chanting loudly and waving signs.

"Grandma, I don't believe this!" Shana cried. "We can't go out there!"

"Of course we can," Edith said. "You see? There are police barricades holding them back."

"Yes, but they sound so angry—and look at their signs!" Painted on them were the slogans "Edith sells out!" and "'Glitters' is Garbage: Don't do it, Edith!"

"Never mind the signs," Edith ordered, adjusting her pearls. "They can't hurt anyone. Just smile and ignore them."

"Oh, right." How can we ignore a hundred furious fans? she wondered.

The driver hurried around and opened the door. Edith stepped out. A blizzard of flashes went off. The chanting grew louder. Shana's knees were trembling, but she followed close behind her grandmother.

Half a dozen reporters rushed up. Shana cringed, but it was her grandmother they wanted to interview. Thrusting their microphones forward, they peppered her with questions: Why had she made the switch from "Children" to "Glitters?" For money? How did she feel about the sexy scenes on her new show?

Shana watched and grudgingly admired her grandmother as she fielded the questions. It took a lot of nerve to stay cool in that type of situation, Shana had to admit. Although now that she was outside the limo, she could see that the crowd wasn't so large as it had looked at first. And the reporters weren't really out for blood—they just wanted a good story.

Shifting her weight from foot to foot, she began to wish they would ask *her* a question. After all, she told herself, I've been on the show for an entire year. Why should Edith get all the attention?

Just then, the show's producer rushed out of the studio entrance. "Welcome, Edith!" Sally Conners cried, brushing past Shana without so much as a nod. "We're delighted to see you! Won't you come inside?"

Turning to the reporters, Sally dismissed them with a wave, obviously anxious to cut off their pointed questions. So much for free speech, Shana thought, annoyed.

Linking arms, Sally and Edith headed for the studio doors. Boos and cheers followed them.

Edith frowned. "Come along, Shana," she said almost as an afterthought.

"Come along, Shana," Shana mimicked under her breath. Was she a pet poodle, or what?

Inside, she trailed behind as the two older women made their way toward the dressing rooms. Why is everyone ignoring me? she wondered. First the reporters had excluded her, and now Sally was giving her the cold shoulder as well. Didn't she count for anything anymore?

Evidently not. When they reached Edith's dressing room, her grandmother and Sally disappeared inside and shut the door without even a backward glance. It was a deliberate snub, she decided. Obviously, neither one cared about her feelings at all.

Furious, she marched down the hall to her own dressing room. Shana whipped the door open—and stopped short.

Her friend Katie Nolan was sitting inside, a mischievous sparkle in her clear green eyes.

"Katie! What are you doing here? You're off this week," Shana said, feeling a grin spread across her face.

Katie smiled, pushing her shoulder-length blond hair behind her ears. "I came in to give you moral support."

"Wow, am I ever glad you did!"

"I bet. Last week you sounded so down about your grandmother's premiere that I was wondering if you'd survive."

Shana groaned. "So far, so bad. I'm afraid it's going to get worse too. But with you around things seem less hopeless."

Settling in front of her mirror, Shana studied her friend. Katie was a beautiful actress: blond, slender, and blessed with all-American good looks. A newcomer to the "Glitters" cast, she was also an awesome talent. In her role as Alicia Gately, teen vixen, she had—in six short weeks—become one of the most popular characters on the show.

Not that Katie's life had always been so charmed—far from it! When she had started on the show, her role had been only temporary. To make it permanent, she had had to prove herself to Sally Conners and overcome her father's resistance to the part. She had done it, though, and now, after a one-week breather, she would be coming back on the show for good.

Shana was happy about that. Not only was Katie terrific to work with, she was also one of the best friends Shana had ever had. From the first second they had met, something clicked between them. Now they were inseparable—two crazy loons bouncing off each other and giving each other support.

"So, your grandmother's giving you trouble already, huh?" Katie asked.

"You can say that again!" Shana began to unbraid her hair.

"What's she doing?"

"Oh, the usual—messing in my career every chance she gets. I mean, can you believe it? This morning she even told me what to wear!" She plucked disdainfully at her dress.

Katie giggled. "You know, I was wondering—that's nice, but it doesn't look like you."

"No way! I wouldn't wear this to a funeral!"

"So why didn't you tell her that?" Katie asked.

She shook her head. "You don't know Edith. Once she gets an idea into her head, dynamite won't tear it loose. If I had argued, she would have gone into a rage."

There was a short silence while Katie digested this information. "Hmmm," she said finally. "Sounds like she's a real problem."

Shana began to pull her brush through her hair. "Yeah, and now me and my problem are going to be working together every day. Whoopee!"

"Come on—it won't be that bad."

"No? How would you like it if your parents hung out here every day, watching you work?"

"I wouldn't like it at all," Katie admitted. "But that's not the point. What I meant was, you and she won't work together *all* the time. You'll only be in certain episodes together."

Shana thought a minute. "I guess you're right," she conceded. "All That Glitters" had many plots going at any given time, so often two actresses would not be in the studio on the same days. In fact, if the rotation of story lines worked out right, they could miss each other for a week or longer.

"You *are* in different story lines, aren't you?" Katie asked.

Shana nodded. The scripts for that week introduced Edith's character, Betty Balfour, an amnesiac, in a plot that had nothing at all to do with Shana's character, Jasmin Palavi.

Of course, there would be days like that first day when their stories would coincide on a single episode, Shana reminded herself. Working with Edith once in a while would be unavoidable. But probably they would see each other in the studio only two or three days a week. Feeling a little better, she gave Katie a weak smile.

Suddenly Edith herself appeared in the door. "Shana! I thought I asked you to—oh, pardon me," she said, seeing Katie. "You have a guest."

"Grandma, this is Katie Nolan," Shana explained. "Katie, my grandmother."

Katie's eyes widened at the sight of the famous Edith Bradbury. "P-pleased to meet you," she said in a hushed voice.

"And you too." Edith squinted as if recognizing Katie for the first time. "Oh, yes—you are Alicia Gately. You do a highly convincing vixen, young lady."

"Thanks." Katie blushed furiously at the unexpected praise.

"Now, will you please excuse us?" Edith commanded. "I want to have a word with Shana."

"Sure thing. 'Bye, Shana. I'll talk to you later," Katie said, hurrying out the door.

When Katie was gone, Edith shut the dressing room door. She began to pace up and down, a stern look on her face.

"I don't like that young woman," she snapped at last. "In the future, Shana, I hope you will think twice about associating with her."

Shana was stunned by the sudden reversal in Edith's attitude. "What do you mean! Katie's the best friend I have in the world."

"Oh? I wonder. She strikes me as an ambitious sort. I'm afraid she'll try to take advantage of you, one day."

"Katie would never do that."

"Don't be so sure," her grandmother advised. "Deceit has many faces."

Shana's jaw tightened in anger. In addition to everything else, Edith was now insulting her friends! Before she blew up, she reminded herself that they were in different story lines and wouldn't be working together often. Edith would only be on her case a few days a week. Tapping her foot, she calmed herself.

"What was it you wanted?" she asked.

Her grandmother's face lit up. "I have wonderful news! I just finished my meeting with Sally Conners, and she tells me that the show's writers have accepted a suggestion I made."

"Suggestion?"

"In fact, they love it." Edith beamed. "Starting next week you and I will be the stars of an exciting joint story line. It will run every day. We'll be working together constantly."

"W-working together?" Suddenly Shana felt weak.

"Yes, isn't it marvelous? Why, we'll even be able to rehearse at home!"

Two

★

Shana went through the rest of the day in shock. She felt like a zombie, her limbs moving in slow motion. Only one thing kept her going: her date that evening with Mitch Callahan, the male lead of "All That Glitters."

Mitch wasn't in that day's episode, so he was at home in his downtown SoHo loft. They had arranged to meet in front of a restaurant near his loft, and she rushed to hail a taxi as soon as the final taping was over. The taxi seemed to take an eternity to plow through the after-work traffic. But finally, breathless and tense, she arrived.

Mitch was leaning against a building, looking cool and relaxed in a pair of faded jeans and a khaki shirt that had seen better days. Shana loved his easygoing style. It was a wonderful contrast to his handsome, dark looks and devastating crystal blue eyes. Leaping out of the taxi, she tossed a five-dollar bill through the driver's window and ran to Mitch, her hair flying.

"Hey, what's wrong?" Mitch asked as she threw her arms around him. "You look like you just met your executioner."

"That's pretty close," she said, hugging him as tightly as she could.

They stayed that way for a minute, Mitch's strong arms around her, his hand stroking her hair. Shana felt herself calming at his touch. Mitch could be difficult at times, especially in the studio—his acting was quite often brilliant but he did give in to fits of moody anger. There was a story around the studio that he had once been arrested for burglary, and though Shana dismissed it as spiteful rumor, she wondered if the arrest charge had a grain of truth. Right then, though, he was at his most gentle.

Finally she lifted her head for a kiss. Mitch obliged, but it was not the soul-melting exchange she had needed.

He drew back, a smile pulling at the corners of his mouth. "So what's up? Did your closet catch on fire or something?"

"Ha-ha."

She gave him a swat on the arm. Mitch loved to tease her about her obsession with clothes. He found her marathon shopping sprees weird. But, she thought, what could you expect from a guy whose idea of dressing up was putting on a Hawaiian-print shirt and Wayfarer sunglasses?

"Seriously," Mitch said, "did all your other stuff vaporize or what? That dress you're wearing isn't you at all."

Shana glanced down at her dress and made a face. "My grandmother made me wear it. She wanted me to look professional for her premiere on the show."

"Oh, I get it—that's why you're so freaked out. It's because of Edith."

Shana nodded. "She's a monster! Do you know what she did? She had me put into her plot line. Now I'll have to do scenes with her. She says we'll even rehearse at home!"

"Don't worry about it. It'll probably be okay," Mitch assured her. But that was all he said.

"Yeah, right," Shana mumbled. She was disappointed. Obviously, Mitch didn't understand her problem the way Katie had.

Looking away, she twisted a strand of hair around her finger. Why was it so hard for Mitch to understand how she was feeling?

When she looked at him again, a change had come over him. His smile was gone, and his eyes were focused in the distance. He turned his head and gestured toward the restaurant. "Let's get something to eat, okay?"

"I'm not hungry," Shana told him. "Could we walk instead?"

Mitch nodded. "Sure. Maybe that's better anyway. I want to talk."

A pang of apprehension shot through Shana. He had mentioned a "talk" when he had asked her out the week before. About what, he hadn't said, but she could guess. He wanted to know if they were ever going to stop merely dating and start getting serious.

She had been debating that very point herself lately. On the one hand, she liked Mitch. He was kind and considerate—and a terrific kisser to boot. When he held her close, she felt as if she were floating. But on the other hand, she was frightened of him at times. He had a side that was moody and quick to anger.

Taking his hand, she walked with him up West Broadway. A late-afternoon shower had cooled the air and left a damp sheen on the sidewalks and buildings. As they walked, Shana thought about what she would tell him.

Part of her, she knew, wasn't ready to get serious with anyone. She had been dating since she was fourteen; she liked boys and they liked her too. Friends like Katie were in awe of her easy friendships with guys. But she had never found it easy to let a boy get close to her—either physically or emotionally. Most of the guys she met were young actors; they were usually more eager to get their careers established than to tie themselves down with a relationship. They had to be ready to pack up at a moment's notice if they got a part in a show or film. Shana had learned that it wasn't wise to give her heart to someone who had already made up his mind that his resumé was more important than she was.

Mitch was as ambitious as any other actor. Shana knew it would be tough to get close with him. But she wanted to try. She needed his support because of her problems with Edith.

Yes, she thought, I just have to stay with Mitch! I need him, I really do.

Her mind was made up. She opened her mouth to introduce the subject of their relationship.

But just then Mitch squeezed her hand. "Shana, did you ever know someone, but felt like you didn't really know them at all?"

"Uh-huh." She nodded. That was exactly how she felt about him. He was easy to be with, yet he was so mysterious too.

"Well, sometimes that's how I feel about you."

"Me?"

"Yeah," he said. "Like when we're kissing— for a while you really get into it, but when things start to get—well, heavier, you back off."

"I have a right to do that, don't I?"

"Sure. That's not what bothers me. It's that I don't know *why*. Every time I try to talk to you about it you crack a joke. Either that, or you change the subject."

"Well, what about you?" she snapped back. "You're worse. Every time I ask you about your past, you close up like a clam."

"See what I mean? You just changed the subject."

Shana stared at him, then giggled. "You're right, I did. I'm sorry. Kissing and stuff like that is hard for me to talk about."

"Me, too, if you want to know the truth," Mitch admitted.

Shana was surprised by that. She had always assumed that he had had a lot of experience in that department—a lot more than she had anyway.

"That's something we'll have to learn to talk about together," she said, feeling a mixture of anxiety and relief.

"Uh—maybe," Mitch said, looking uncomfortable.

"What?"

"I mean, that's not the only thing I wanted to bring up," he continued. "I also think we're very different people."

Shana laughed. "You can say *that* again!"

"I'm serious," he insisted. "We come from such different worlds. Your family has money and connections, and mine—well, let's just say I grew up on the street."

"Come on, Mitch, you don't really believe that matters, do you?"

"In a way, yeah. That's not the only difference either. You like to dance and party, and I don't. You have tons of friends, but I'm a loner. We have different styles."

"What's wrong with that? I *like* our differences. They're what makes us special together. They're part of the fun."

Mitch shook his head. "Relationships aren't just fun. They're a lot of things—like having common interests."

Turning a corner, they started down a quieter side street. Shana was worried by the direction the conversation was taking. Was he saying that he wanted her to become more like him? That didn't seem fair. Or wise either. She was who she was.

She had a sudden inspiration. "Mitch, we'll find stuff we like to do together. In fact, I just thought of something we can do right now. . . ."

Stopping, she turned and wrapped her arms around him. Then slowly she touched his lips with a soft kiss. People were passing on either side of them, but she didn't care. She only wanted things to be the way they had been with her and Mitch. His mood was beginning to scare her.

"Shana—"

He tried to unwrap her arms from around his neck. She clung tighter, beginning to panic.

"Shana!" This time he was angry. He pushed her away roughly. "Cut it out, all right? I'm trying to be serious."

"So am *I*," she cried. "Look, you said before that I always back off when we kiss. Well, this time I won't!" She tossed her hair defiantly.

Mitch shook his head. "That's not what I want."

"*What?*"

Shana's mouth dropped open. I can't be hearing right, she thought. Sure, sometimes I get scared, I pull away. But I've never had a guy pull away from me—especially Mitch.

"I'm—I don't understand," she said in a shaky voice. "What *are* we talking about?"

"Not dating each other anymore," Mitch told her. "I'm sorry, Shana. I should have come right out and said that earlier, but I didn't know how."

Suddenly the world began spinning around her. Shana heard a loud buzzing in her ears. Am I crazy? she wondered. Did Mitch really just announce that he wants to break up?

"Shana? Are you all right?" he asked when she didn't speak.

"I think I'd better sit down," she said.

Quickly Mitch led her to a nearby set of steps.

"It's not that I don't like you, or anything," he was saying. "It's just that I don't think we're right for each other."

"But what about all the fun things we've done? Are you telling me you haven't enjoyed the time we've spent together?"

"Sure, I have, but—"

"But what?" Her voice rose in a panicky wail. "You like me, we have fun together—what else is there? I don't understand!"

Mitch ran his fingers through his hair. "Shana, there has to be more than that for a relationship to work. There has to be—I don't know—a kind of spark, I guess."

Tears were beginning to pool in her eyes and spill down her cheeks. Wiping them away, Shana thought about how wonderful she felt when he kissed her. You couldn't exactly call that feeling a "spark," but it was awfully close. "We have plenty of that," she said.

A guilty look came into his eyes. "Yes and no. I mean, sure, we turn each other on, but that's not the same as . . ."

"As what?"

"Love."

Her tears began to flow faster than she could wipe them away. She had always known that he didn't love her. She didn't love him either—not in the deepest sense. But hearing him say it out loud hurt so much. She had been hoping their feelings would grow as they spent more time together. She sniffed loudly.

Mitch took a handkerchief from his shirt pocket and handed it to her. He looked sad, but not sad enough to change his mind.

"I'm sorry," he said.

Suddenly, with a jolt so sharp she actually jumped, Shana realized why love had become so important to him. "You're in love with another girl, aren't you?" she demanded.

Mitch looked startled. He didn't answer, but she could tell from the way he was avoiding her eyes that she had guessed correctly. Anger blazed up inside her.

"How could you go out with someone else and not tell me?" she demanded.

"I haven't!"

"No? Then why can't you look at me? Who is she?"

Again Mitch remained silent.

Shana seethed. So! Maybe he hadn't been dating this other girl, but she existed, no question. Furious, she leapt up from the steps and threw his handkerchief at him.

"For three months I've been waiting for something to happen between us! But nothing ever did. And now I know why."

Mitch objected. "Wait a minute. It wasn't only my fault that things never really clicked. You held back too."

He was right, of course, but Shana was too angry to admit it. She couldn't stand the idea of some other girl filling his fantasies. Not now, she thought. Not when I need him so much! She stamped her foot.

"Mitch Callahan, I think you're a low, contemptible toad!"

"That's not fair, Shana. I've always been honest with you. Even now."

"You call running around behind my back honest?"

"I'm not—"

"Of course you're not. You're just in love. It happened by magic, I suppose?"

A glazed look came into his eyes as if he were remembering a special time and place. "Yeah, it was a little like that."

Shana couldn't stand it. It was over. Dead. Extinct. The guy whom she had been counting on to rescue her from Edith was dumping her for someone else.

How will I make it through the next few weeks alone? she thought, anguished. Mitch doesn't even care whether I do or not!

She turned abruptly and walked away. "Shana!" Mitch called. She began walking faster, then broke into a run as she heard his footsteps behind her. There could be no turning back to him ever again, she realized.

★

Three

"Come on, Shana, *try*. If you don't learn your lines by tomorrow, you're only going to make a fool of yourself and get into trouble."

Listlessly, Shana fell back among the pillows at the head of Katie's bed. She didn't want to learn her lines. She didn't care if she got in trouble or made a fool of herself either. She felt like a world-class idiot already. How could I have trusted that creep? she asked herself for the hundredth time. How could I have been so dumb?

Next to Shana on the bedside table, Katie's alarm clock flashed the time in big red numbers. It's been exactly twenty-six hours and ten minutes since Mitch and I broke up, Shana noted. Why

25

does it still hurt so much? Shouldn't some of the pain have worn off by now?

"Shana?" Katie asked. She was sitting across the room on her pink-cushioned window seat, the script for the next day open in her lap. "Are you okay? Do you want an aspirin, or anything?"

Shana shook her head. "No, thanks. What I really need is to have my head examined. Why did I let myself get involved with him in the first place, Katie? I should have known!"

Katie sighed in resignation and closed the script.

"Shana, you didn't know he was going to dump you when you started out. How could you have known that?"

Shana shrugged. "I don't know. Maybe because he's so mysterious about things. Like his loft. Did I tell you he never took me there?"

"I know. You mentioned it before."

"I mean, he never even *tried*!" she wailed, ignoring Katie's remark. "Do you think I just didn't—you know, turn him on?"

"Oh, Shana!" Katie said. "You're so gorgeous, how can you think that?"

"Well, then, what went wrong?"

"I don't know. He's a funny guy. . . ." Katie's voice trailed off. Looking down, she flipped the pages of Shana's script a few times.

Shana studied her friend. Why is Katie defending Mitch? she wondered. Even though she played opposite Mitch on the show, Katie claimed they didn't get along.

Or did they? All at once Shana recalled that it was Katie who had discovered that Mitch coached kids' wheelchair basketball. And it was Katie, not her, whom Mitch had told about his one-time job mopping floors in a midtown skyscraper. If they didn't get along, then how come Katie knew more about him than his own girlfriend? Her heart began to pound.

But, no—it couldn't be. Quickly, she calmed herself. Katie wasn't the kind of friend who would run around behind her back. Katie was honest and loyal. If anything was going on between her and Mitch, she would have come right out and said so.

Relaxing, she glanced around Katie's room. She hadn't really taken the time to study it before. She had always known that it was warm and cozy. The colors were all soft pastels, the bed and dresser antiques, and there was a shelf of plays and acting textbooks over a well-used desk. She loved it. It was so—so *normal*. In comparison, her room in the Bradbury townhouse was a mausoleum.

"I'm glad you invited me over," she said, turning back to Katie. "If I'd had to go home after work today I think I would have totally lost my grip on reality."

"No problem." Katie shrugged.

"Really, I mean it. Talking to you helps a lot. You're a great friend."

Katie blushed and looked down again. "Was it rough seeing Mitch in the studio today?"

"Is Häagen-Dazs ice cream fattening?"
Shana shot back. Her heart constricted as she
remembered. "Half the time I wanted to deck
him, and the other half I wanted to cry. It was
horrible. I felt like I was being whipped around in
a blender at high speed."

"I can imagine," Katie said sympathetically.

"It's funny, though—you know who I'm
madder at than Mitch?"

"No, who?"

"His new girlfriend," she said bitterly. "I *hate*
her! Girls who steal guys are the lowest form of
life on the planet."

Katie looked confused. "Wait a minute—I
thought Mitch said he wasn't dating anyone
else."

Shana narrowed her eyes. "That's what he
said, but I don't believe it. How could he fall in
love if he wasn't?"

"Are you sure he's in love?"

"Positive. I could tell from his expression.
Guys don't look that dopey-eyed unless they've
been hooked."

Katie's face had gone white. "Who do you
think this other girl is?"

"I don't know. But I'll tell you one thing, if I
ever find out who she is, I'll scratch her eyes out!"

Katie broke the tension with a laugh. "Well, we
know how you feel about that subject. How about
a little music?" she asked. Without waiting for an
answer, she went to her stereo and flipped it on.
Music blasted from the speakers.

"Hey, Katie"—Shana raised her voice in order to be heard above the music—"I didn't mean to upset you too!"

Katie giggled and turned down the volume. "Don't worry, I'm fine." She crossed the room and gave Shana a warm hug. "You're the one we've got to get back on her feet."

Hugging Katie back, Shana wondered whether that would ever happen. Right then it didn't feel like it. It felt as if the ground underneath her had turned to ice. First Edith, then Mitch—every time she took a step she slipped.

It helped to know that Katie would be there for her. But she had a nagging feeling that even Katie wasn't being straight with her.

On Saturday Shana bounded into the breakfast room at two minutes past eleven. Normally she would not have been up so early on a weekend, but today she felt good. The reason was Saks Fifth Avenue. The department store was having a huge one-day sale, and as a reward to herself for surviving a week of misery, she was going to buy them out.

The moment she entered the room, however, her bouncy mood evaporated. Edith was sitting at the table. A script was open in front of her, and she was making notes in its margins.

"Grandma! Why are you still here?" she asked in surprise.

It was unusual to find Edith in the breakfast room at that hour. She rose early on Saturdays and was usually gone by now.

"I'm waiting for you," Edith said, pulling off her reading glasses.

Shana slipped into her seat with a nervous cough. It looked bad. What had she done wrong? Had her latest credit card bills arrived?

"This afternoon you and I will rehearse the scene we are doing together on Monday," Edith announced.

Shana's jaw dropped. On Thursday they had received their scripts for the coming week, and, as promised, there were several scenes between her character and Edith's. But she hadn't expected the at-home rehearsals to begin this soon!

"We can't rehearse now," she objected. "I was planning to go to Saks."

"Your plans will have to wait," her grandmother informed her.

"*Grand*-ma! Couldn't we do it another time, please?"

"No," Edith insisted. "This afternoon is it. Tonight I'm attending a concert, and tomorrow I will be meeting all day with our accountants."

"How about Monday morning after breakfast?" Shana asked, bargaining.

Edith didn't even bother to answer. Instead, she returned her reading glasses to her face and resumed making notes. The discussion was over.

Cursing under her breath, Shana dumped milk on her cornflakes. What a drag! she thought.

Now I'm going to miss some of the biggest bargains of the century! The rehearsal wouldn't be long, of course—their Monday scene was short—but by the time she got to the store the best things would be gone.

Chewing the soggy flakes, she wondered if she could worm her way out of it. No way, she decided. Edith had used her school principal voice—a sure sign that her mind was made up. No, the only way out was to cooperate. She'd give it her best effort and hope that Edith would let her go quickly.

"Ready?" Edith asked when Shana had finished eating.

"Ready." *As I'll ever be*, she added to herself.

Edith led her into the front parlor. Like the rest of the Bradbury townhouse on Sutton Place, it was impressive, with sixteen-foot ceilings, turn-of-the-century furniture, and tall french windows. Visitors gasped when they saw it, but Shana was so used to it she barely glanced around the room.

Edith handed her the script so Shana could read the scene. Shana scanned it and memorized her lines on the spot. It wasn't hard to do. She only had five.

Then they began. In no time they had run through the scene once, then twice. At the end of the second run-through, Shana looked at her grandmother questioningly. It had sounded good to her. Surely Edith would be satisfied, too.

Her grandmother shook her head. "No, no— you're missing every nuance. Take another look at it."

Shana opened the script again and read the scene. It looked the same to her as it had on a first reading. It was a simple request for help from Edith's character, Betty Balfour, and a promise from her own character, Jasmin Palavi, to help Betty. What was so subtle about that?

They ran through it once more. Still Edith was not satisfied.

"Shana, can't you see what's happening in this scene?"

"Sure! Jasmin's agreeing to help Betty."

"Correct—but why?"

Suddenly Shana saw what her grandmother was trying to do. Anger welled up inside her. Edith was treating her like a baby—or worse, like a first year acting student! She was insulted.

"Come on, Grandma, don't try to tell me that I don't understand motivation. I've been acting for twelve years, remember?"

"Okay, then, what *is* Jasmin's motivation in this scene?" Edith asked.

"How should I know! She's only got five lines. 'Yes.' 'Are you kidding?' 'I can't help you.' 'Okay, I'll try.' And 'Yes, I promise.' Who needs motivation to say those?"

Her grandmother sighed. "Shana, as an actress it's your job to find the motivation in every word, no matter how insignificant it seems."

"Okay, okay!"

Shana shut the script with a snap. This was absurd! She was never going to get to Saks at that rate. Still, she had promised herself that she would cooperate, and cooperate she would. Crossing her arms, she thought for a moment.

"All right," she said. "I guess Jasmin agrees to help Betty because she feels sorry for her."

Edith looked pleased. "Good! Now let's try it again."

They ran through the scene. This time there was a difference—a slight one, in Shana's opinion, but a difference nonetheless. Edith was a bit more desperate, and Jasmin was a bit more sympathetic.

"There! You see how we're starting to play off each other?" Edith asked.

"I guess so."

"Now this time I'll make Edith more uncertain. You make Jasmin more curious, and we'll see what happens."

As they worked, Shana gradually began to see the sense in what her grandmother was saying. If she worked at it, even simple lines could convey complex meaning.

She also began to see both their characters more clearly than before. Betty was an amnesiac, a woman with no memory; Jasmin was a seer, an exchange student with psychic powers. They were both women cut loose from their pasts.

"Excellent!" Edith said awhile later. "That time Jasmin was not only sympathetic, she was concerned, too. That was very good."

In spite of herself, Shana felt a little swell of pride. Compliments from her grandmother were rare, and she had earned that one.

"Okay, this time let's try another approach. Let's pretend that Betty doesn't believe in Jasmin's psychic powers. Not only that, let's say that Jasmin doubts them herself. Ready?"

They tried the scene again, and again, and again. When Shana glanced at the clock on the mantle, it was four o'clock. Saks would be closing in an hour!

"Hey! Can't I go now?" she said.

Edith halted in midgesture, an annoyed look on her face. "No, you may not. We still have a long way to go with this."

"Grandma! We've been over it a thousand times. Why do we have to do it again?"

"Because you need to learn that every scene is important, and that every line deserves the very best you can give it."

"Come on, the director is going to give us our readings anyway."

Edith nodded. "Probably, and given the hectic schedule we'll probably use them too. But that's no excuse for being unprepared."

Shana had had all she could take. It was fine to be conscientious, but that was getting ridiculous! It's only "Glitters" we're talking about, after all, she thought. Just a soap!

"I think the reading I just did was good enough." Shana waited for her grandmother to say something. Edith just stared at her. "I want to go now," she added.

Edith exploded. "Go? You're not going anywhere! Young lady, that reading wasn't good enough—it barely qualified as acting! In fact, your entire performance on the show has been slipping lately."

Shana couldn't believe what she was hearing. "Are you telling me you've been *watching* me?"

Edith nodded. "Of course I have. And let me tell you, I'm disturbed by what I've seen. It's high time someone took you in hand and made you *work* for a change."

Shana dropped into a leather wing chair. She felt as if she had been hit. So *that* was why her grandmother had left "Destiny's Children" at such an unusual time! She hadn't joined "All That Glitters" for the money, as everyone thought—she had joined so that she could get directly involved in her granddaughter's career!

"I don't believe this," she muttered.

"Don't believe what, dear?" her grandmother asked.

"That you've been keeping a mental report card on me."

"What's so unusual about that?" Edith shrugged. "You're my granddaughter, and I'm concerned for your welfare. I want you to be happy."

"Yeah, well, rehearsing a dinky little scene over and over again isn't doing much to cheer me up. I'd rather go to Saks!"

Pulling her knees up to her chin, Shana brooded. This whole setup was totally unfair. She didn't need any coaching from her grandmother! She was doing just fine on "Glitters." True, she hadn't been putting her heart into it lately, but what did that matter? No one was complaining.

The next moment she made a decision. She wasn't going to let herself be pushed around! I'm seventeen years old, she told herself—I have a right to do as I please.

She stood up. "Grandma, I appreciate your wanting to help improve my acting and all, but it really isn't necessary."

"You don't think so?"

"No, I don't. So if it's all right with you, I'm going to Saks now." Turning, she marched toward the door.

Edith's voice stopped her cold. "Come back here, young lady. You're not going anywhere until we finish this rehearsal."

"Oh, *yeah*?" Shana whirled around, her own voice rising to a shout. "Well, just try to stop me! You don't control my life!"

"Not completely, but I do control your credit cards," Edith said smoothly. "Your trip to Saks won't be much fun if I cancel them."

Shana froze in horror. "You wouldn't!"

"Wouldn't I?" Edith crossed to the telephone that sat next to the chesterfield sofa and lifted the receiver. "One call and those cards are worthless, Shana. Care to test me?"

"That's blackmail!"

"No, that's my right and my responsibility as your temporary guardian."

Temporary guardian, Shana thought bitterly. As if my mother is ever going to wake up and take over.

A trembling began in her legs and quickly spread to her whole body. "Why are you doing this to me?" she asked, her voice catching in her throat. "Why are you ruining my life?"

The receiver clattered as Edith dropped it back into place. "I'm not trying to ruin your life, Shana. I'm trying to make it better."

"Sure."

"It's true. Listen to me, you won't be playing ingenue roles forever. You're a beautiful young woman, and soon producers will be offering you adult roles. I want to be sure you have the skills to handle them, that's all."

Shana barely heard what her grandmother was saying. She was too angry. It isn't fair! she thought. Other kids don't have Ediths dictating their futures for them. Why should I? Wasn't slavery abolished in the Civil War?

Her grandmother held out the script to her again. Crossing the room, Shana snatched it from her.

They continued to rehearse.

★
Four

The moment she arrived in the studio on Monday morning, Shana went in search of Katie. She found her friend sitting in an unused set, absorbed in a crossword puzzle.

"What's a five-letter word meaning 'sadistic'?" Katie asked as she approached.

Shana supplied the answer in two seconds flat. "Edith!"

Katie giggled. "Hmmm—I don't think that works. The third letter has to be—Hey, you look upset! What's wrong?"

Pacing back and forth, Shana filled her in on Edith's plan to improve her acting skills. As she spoke, she could feel her face getting hot. That didn't surprise her. She had been seething all weekend.

When she had finished, Katie whistled in amazement. "You mean she left 'Destiny's Children' just so she could coach you? That's incredible!"

"Not if you know my grandmother," Shana replied. "She's made a second career out of interfering in my professional life."

"She has?"

"Katie, haven't I ever told you what it was like growing up with her?"

Katie folded her paper. "No, not really. Mostly you've been pretty mysterious about your family. But tell me—I'm dying to know!"

Pulling up a chair, Shana sat down and tried to explain. "I hardly know where to start," she said. "Let's see—maybe with my fifth birthday.

"It was a wonderful day," Shana began. "At first, that is. I got tons of presents. And, afterward, Edith took me to the Central Park Zoo. When we got home, I was happy but really tired. That's when Edith sprang her little trap on me."

"What little trap?"

"She asked me if I'd like to be in a Broadway musical—said it would be a lot of fun, almost like having a birthday every day.

"Naturally, I shouted yes!" Shana told Katie bitterly. "And in no time I was singing and dancing my way through eight performances a week."

"Didn't you enjoy it at all?" Katie asked.

' "Not really. But that didn't matter to my grandmother. All Edith cared about was keeping the family tradition alive.

"One by one, Edith pushed me into new roles. If I complained, she'd make me feel guilty. The public loved me, she'd say. If I didn't act anymore I'd be letting people down. So, before I knew it, I was a child star," Shana finished.

Katie's face was glowing. "That sounds like a fairy tale."

"It's been a nightmare, believe me," Shana replied. "Don't you see? Every step of the way my grandmother has arranged everything. I became a child star, sure, but I had no choice!"

Katie still doesn't understand, Shana thought, looking at her friend's shining face. To her, my life is a dream come true.

"I wish someone like Edith had been around to open all those doors for *me*!" Katie said.

"Well, that's the difference between us. You've wanted to be an actress all your life, but I've never been anything else."

"What *do* you want to be?" Katie asked. "Don't you like acting?"

"Sure, but—" She paused. That was just the trouble. While she knew she wanted to do more with her life, when it came to choosing alternatives her vision became cloudy. What were her choices? How would they feel? The truth was, she didn't know. How could she fight against Edith when she didn't know what she wanted?

"I think you're lucky," Katie said. "I mean, having a pro like your grandmother coaching you is great. She knows so much!"

"Yeah, like how to drive me nuts. Seriously, Katie, what's so great about being forced to work fourteen hours a day, seven days a week? There's more to life than acting."

"There is? Like what?" Katie wanted to know.

"Boys!"

A short silence followed. Katie slid down in her chair and sighed. "Oh, yeah—boys. It would be great to have a boyfriend, wouldn't it?"

"Maybe."

"I'm sorry. I shouldn't have said that." Katie reached over and gave her friend's hand a squeeze. "You're still hurting about Mitch, aren't you?"

"A little."

Actually, it was more than a little. Whenever Shana thought about him—or worse, saw him in the studio—she felt like crying. It was dumb, of course. A week had passed, and she ought to have begun getting over him. But she couldn't. Something inside her wouldn't let go.

"Don't worry, it'll stop hurting soon," Katie said, reading her mind.

"You think so?"

"Sure! I mean, nothing lasts forever. Besides, think of all the other guys who must be waiting for a chance with you. Any minute now one of them could sweep you off your feet."

Shana looked around the nearly empty studio. "Any century now would be more like it. They aren't exactly standing in line."

"Well, maybe not now, but give it time. Another guy will come along."

"I sure hope so. There's nothing like a new romance to help you get over an old one. The problem is, where do I find one?"

"What about that disco you like so much?"

"Outer Space? Yeah, I guess I could go there. But everyone there will know Mitch and I broke up. I don't want to be too obvious." Shana sighed. "Katie, if you could have a guy custom-made for you, what would he be like?"

"My ideal boyfriend?" Katie thought for a minute. "I don't know. He'd be good-looking, for sure. Tall, dark haired, with intense eyes that always looked right at me."

"Sounds like a hypnotist," Shana quipped.

Katie nodded seriously. "Yeah, in a way. When I was with him, I'd feel like I was under a spell. He'd be that special."

"What else?"

"Well, he'd be polite. Fun to talk to. He'd be a great kisser, but not the type who'd pressure me for more."

"A wimp."

"Oh, no! Not at all!" Katie protested. "He'd be strong and self-assured. Maybe even a bit mysterious too."

There was one boy who fit Katie's fantasy perfectly—a boy they both knew. Am I being paranoid? Shana wondered. Raising an eyebrow, she looked at her friend.

"That sounds a lot like Mitch," she said.

Katie turned bright red. "Do you think so? I wasn't thinking of him."

"You could have fooled me. Your description fits him perfectly."

"Shana! Don't be ridiculous. I mean, even if I wanted Mitch for my boyfriend, I'd be an idiot to hope that it would ever happen. Mostly he treats me like I don't exist."

Shana had to admit that that was true. In fact, in the weeks before Katie's role was made permanent, Mitch had been absolutely beastly to her. Nobody in her right mind would want to fall in love with a guy who treated her like that. Nobody except me, Shana thought.

At that moment there was a commotion outside the studio door. Crew and cast members began pouring in from the hallway. For the first time, Shana glanced at her watch. It was late, she saw—long past the time at which the first stage of rehearsal, read-through, usually began. What was going on?

Then, at the center of the crowd coming in, she noticed a boy she had never seen before. Her heart skipped a beat. He was gorgeous! Tall and tan, he had an athletic-looking body and an easy way of moving that she found fascinating. Others were drawn to him, too, apparently. Everyone was talking to him at once.

"Hey, who's that?" she asked Katie.

Her friend had sat up sharply in her chair. "Wow, I don't believe it!"

"Katie—who *is* he?"

"Don't you watch tennis on TV?"

"No, why?" Unlike Katie, who was an avid tennis player, Shana wasn't interested in sports at all.

"Well, if you did, you'd know him. That's Kirk Tucker!"

"Kirk *who*?"

Katie giggled. "Honestly, Shana, you're so out of it sometimes! Kirk Tucker's only the hottest thing to hit the pro tennis tour in years. My dad thinks he's better than John McEnroe."

"John *who*?"

That did it. Katie's giggles dissolved into peals of muffled laughter. Shana was miffed. What's so funny? she wondered. I don't know one tennis player from another—big deal. No one ever told me they were hunks like Kirk!

Just then Alan Asher, one of the cast members, walked by. Robust and white haired, he was impossible to miss. On the show he played overbearing Lionel Davidson, the father of Mitch's character, Matt Davidson.

Katie stopped him. "Alan, what's Kirk Tucker doing here?"

"He's making a guest appearance on today's episode," Alan informed them. "Can you believe it? Eighteen years old, and he's already won the French Open and been in the semi-finals at Wimbledon."

"I don't get it," Katie said. "He's not in the script."

"Sally just lined him up last week. They're adding him to the picnic scene."

That day's script called for a large family gathering at the Davidson mansion. It was during that scene that Katie's character, devilish Alicia Gately, was due to make her reappearance on the show.

Shana asked, "How was Sally able to get him on? Aren't tennis players always flying around the world for tournaments?"

"Kirk's in New York for a charity event, I think," Alan asked.

Katie nodded. "That's right. The pro-celebrity doubles tournament at Forest Hills in two weeks, right?"

"That's the one."

As Alan walked away, Shana's heart began to pound. It was weird, she thought. Ten minutes earlier she had been down in the dumps over Mitch. Now, suddenly seeing Kirk Tucker, she was soaring. I want to meet him, she thought.

She stood and began to move toward the crowd that was still gathered around him. Katie called, "Hey, where are you going?"

"Katie, don't laugh. I think I just saw my ideal guy," Shana said.

Meeting Kirk Tucker didn't prove to be that
easy. As Shana approached the group, Francine
Epps, the head of the makeup crew, appeared
and whisked Kirk away. Shana was disappointed,
but she knew there would be other opportunities
to meet him. Final taping of the episode probably
wouldn't be over until dinnertime.

Her next chance came during a mid-morning
break in dry blocking or read through. The big
picnic scene was half done when the assistant
director, Stu Weintraub, announced a halt. Shana
headed straight for Kirk. Unfortunately, so did
most of the rest of the cast. He was surrounded in
seconds by actors who wanted tips to help
improve their tennis game. She didn't even get
close to him.

After that, her scene with Edith was called.
Then there was lunch. Shana hoped to catch him
again during dress rehearsal, but she didn't even
see him again until midafternoon, just before
doing the picnic scene. That time she was in luck.
He was heading for the set—alone. Like a rocket
she took after him.

"Excuse me, I—"

Just as she was about to catch his arm, a
hairdresser appeared from nowhere and began to
fuss with his golden blond hair. Shana clenched her
teeth. It was getting ridiculous. Was she ever
going to get him alone?

Fuming, she took her place for the start of the
scene. As she did, Kirk also took his place on the

opposite side of the set. Their eyes met, and for one dazzling instant an electric spark seemed to jump between them. Kirk smiled. Shana smiled back, feeling herself melt inside. Now she had to meet him. She *had* to!

Final taping began a short while later. It was the most crucial part of the day. Tension was high, and the studio was dead silent. Any little noise— even a dropped pencil—could be picked up by the boom mikes, spoiling the take. Shana gave her scenes all her concentration, hoping Edith would be satisfied with her interpretation of them.

When the picnic scene was finally over, Shana took off, pushing through the cast and crew, stepping over electrical cables. She was determined to get to Kirk. She spotted him heading through the door to the dressing rooms and followed.

By the time she caught up with him, he was turning into his dressing room. Shana began to panic. What could she do? Once he got out of makeup and costume, he would probably take off. Her last opportunity would be gone. She could wait out in the corridor for him, she knew, but that would look silly. She wasn't a dog.

He shut the door behind him. Making an instant decision, she boldly stepped up, opened the door, and followed him inside.

Kirk was peeling off his tennis shirt. Startled, he whirled around. "What the—"

"H-hi!" she said brightly. She tried to sound cool, but she could feel her heart thumping a thousand miles an hour. "I just wanted to tell you that—uh, that I thought you were really fantastic just now. You could be an actor."

She felt totally foolish. His small part in the picnic scene had only called for him to compliment Lionel Davidson, Alan Asher's character, on his tennis game. What had ever possessed her to do this? If he pushed her out the door, she wouldn't blame him.

He didn't though. "Oh, it's you!"

"Yep, it's me," she confirmed. What a dumb thing to say! Wanting to die, she stuck out her hand. "My name's Shana."

"I know. I'm Kirk," he said, shaking it.

"I hope you don't mind my barging in here like this."

He chuckled. "You surprised me a little, but, no, I don't mind. I was hoping to meet you."

"Y-you were?"

"Yeah, I asked Mr. Asher who you were. He told me and said I should introduce myself, but—I don't know. Somehow I couldn't work up the nerve."

Shana was stunned. She couldn't believe it! All day he had been trying to meet her too! Alan Asher, bless you, she thought.

"I meant what I said a second ago. I thought you were great." She smiled.

"Thanks," he said. "Boy, was I nervous though. I can't imagine how you do this every day! It would drive me nuts."

"You get used to it."

"Going nuts?"

"No, silly," she said, giggling. "Performing!"

For a moment they just smiled at each other. Shana found herself thinking how nice he was. She liked his slight southern accent. And what terrific eyes he had! They were blue and danced with an inner fire. She knew hardly anything about him, yet already she could sense that he was a guy who did things his own way.

Her breath quickened as he held out a chair. "Can you sit and talk for a minute?" he asked.

"Sure—but let's go to my dressing room. Somebody may run in here looking for you." Shana giggled again.

As they settled down in her dressing room, Shana felt comfortable and excited at the same time. She was attracted to Kirk in a very big way, she knew. And she suspected it was mutual.

"What will you do with the rest of your two weeks in New York?" she asked.

He sighed. "Train, mostly. Doesn't matter where I go, I've still got to stay in shape. The tour's brutal."

"Sounds rotten," she said.

"You get used to it."

They both laughed.

"Seriously," he continued, "I do hope to see a little of the city while I'm here. To a Florida boy like me, it looks exciting."

"Well, I'm sure"—she paused, suddenly struck with an idea—"wait a minute, why don't *I* show you the town?"

"Sure! Sounds great!" He seized her suggestion enthusiastically. "Tonight?"

"I can't! I have to learn lines," she groaned.
"How about tomorrow night, though? I'm free
then."

She wasn't actually. There were more lines to
learn for Wednesday. But she'd work it out, she
promised herself. This chance was too good to
pass up!

"Tomorrow night is great."

He quickly wrote down the name of his hotel
and left after taking her phone number. Shana
stared in her mirror, her eyes open wide. She
couldn't believe her luck—the cutest guy she had
met in her entire life, and she was going out with
him! It was incredible! Fantastic! Unbelievable!

Maybe Katie was right, she thought. Maybe it
was only a matter of time.

Five

"Shana, don't you think you're going just a teeny bit overboard?"

Shana barely heard Katie's protest on the other end of the line. She was too happy to listen to any negative remarks right then. Tucking the receiver under her ear, she went dancing across the room, blowing on her fingernails. Why did the darn things take so long to dry?

"Shana, are you listening to me?"

"Nope."

"I said, I think you may be expecting too much from this date."

"Not a chance." She didn't believe that for a minute. "This is going to be the greatest night of my whole life."

In just half an hour she was going to collect Kirk at his hotel. From there, they were going to dinner and then to Outer Space to dance the night away. It was going to be wonderful, no matter what Katie had said. And why not? She, Shana Bradbury, had planned it down to the last detail.

"Shana, I'm worried about you. I don't want you to be disappointed," Katie continued.

"I won't. Stop being such a downer, okay? Let me enjoy myself."

Katie sighed. "I'm sorry. I guess you're right. It's your date—so tell me, what are you wearing? I'll bet it's fantastic."

Shana smiled. "It is. I'm wearing a little black silk dress with an oversized white satin shirt over it. I have tons of silver on each arm and textured black stockings. My hair is teased out and loose, and I have this super expensive shimmery makeup and blush."

"Sounds really—"

"But what kind of perfume should I wear?" she asked, interrupting Katie. "Should I tease him with something innocent or knock him dead with something hot?"

Katie cleared her throat. "Um—I don't know, Shana. It sounds to me like you could already kill at ten paces. Why not skip the perfume?"

"No way!"

Still holding the phone, Shana danced back to her vanity and picked up a tiny atomizer. Yes, that one would do. It was the latest designer perfume, and, if the ads were to be believed, it would instantly sap Kirk's willpower and make him her slave. Gleefully, she spritzed a little on all the right places.

Finally she flopped into a chair with the telephone and surveyed her room. It was a large and drafty place—not at all like Katie's. She had cozied it up a little with a thick cream-colored carpet, a canopied bed, and an entertainment center, but even so it felt impersonal. Especially tonight.

"I'm so nervous. Do you think he'll like the way I look?" she asked Katie.

"I think it's more important that he likes *you*," her friend said, hedging.

Shana groaned. "I knew it. You think I'm overdressed, don't you?"

"Maybe just a little."

"Don't say that! I really want to impress him."

"I know, but you don't have to do anything special to do that. Just be yourself. I mean, Kirk's a tennis star, and all, but underneath he strikes me as a pretty simple guy."

"You *talked* to him!" she screeched. She couldn't believe it!

"Sure. On the way out to lunch. He's really nice, Shana."

"W-what did he say to you?" Her sudden anxiety showed in her voice. They were both blond and beautiful—the perfect couple.

Katie giggled. "He told me to keep my elbow up when I make a backhand volley. Hey, you didn't think I was flirting with him, did you?"

"Me?" Shana let out her breath in relief. "Of course not."

"Good. You didn't have to worry anyway. Jocks aren't my type."

"He's not a jock. He's smart!" Shana leapt to his defense.

"A guy can be smart and still be a jock. What I meant was—oh, never mind. You have to get going soon, don't you?"

Shana glanced at her bedside clock. "Yeah."

"Where are you taking him?"

Briefly she explained her plans for the evening. Katie paused significantly.

"Hmmm—aren't those places that you used to go with Mitch?"

Shana grinned. "They happen to be my favorite places. But I can just picture the look on Mitch's face if he sees me with Kirk. He'll be green!"

"Actually, I was only kidding," Katie said. "You probably won't see Mitch around anyway. Didn't you say he doesn't like clubs anymore?"

"True. From what I've heard he doesn't go *anywhere* anymore." It was one of the strangest things about him, in her opinion.

Katie's voice suddenly became bitter. "Too bad. I'd love to see him suffer."

"Katie!" Shana was shocked. That kind of statement wasn't like Katie at all.

"Sorry. Forget I said that. I didn't mean it, really."

"Then why—?"

"You've got to go, Shana. Have fun. And tell me about it in the morning!"

The receiver buzzed in her ear. Katie had hung up!

What had gotten into that girl? Shana wondered. Why would she, of all people want to see Mitch suffer? After all, it wasn't *her* heart that he had broken. Very strange . . .

But I have more important things to think about than Mitch, she reminded herself. Like Kirk. He's expecting me at any minute! Jumping up, she gave a final, satisfied twirl in front of her mirror, grabbed her purse and headed for the door.

Their first stop would be the Hard Rock Cafe. It was the place to begin a glamorous evening. From its unusual canopy outside—the back end of a fifties Cadillac—to the neon and guitar-decorated walls inside, it was totally New York. Even Kirk looked impressed as they were shown to their table.

Shana was relieved. The truth was, Kirk had been acting distracted ever since they had met in the lobby of his hotel. Talking to him, she had the feeling that he wasn't totally *there*. What was wrong?

Once they were seated, she waved a hand in front of his eyes. "Yo, Kirk! This is your date calling—are you in?"

He snapped his head up, startled. "Huh? Were you saying something?"

"No, I just wanted your attention." She smiled.

"I'm sorry. I guess I've got training on the brain," he admitted.

"Training?"

"Yeah, you see this tour is really competitive. To keep up, I've got to stay in top shape. Good workouts, plenty of sleep—that sort of thing."

"So?"

"So"—He hesitated before blurting out his answer—"I'm beginning to feel a little guilty about this date."

Shana froze. What was he saying? Was he trying to back out? "Look, Kirk, if you have to leave now, I'll unders—"

"No, no! Don't misunderstand me. I'm glad we're going out," he said, reassuring her. "It's just that I can't stay out too late."

Her anxiety began to ease. "Oh, don't worry about that! I have to get to bed early too." It was true, unfortunately. Her call was for seven-thirty, which meant she would have to get home by four in the morning, if not sooner.

"Whew! I'm glad you understand," Kirk said, his relief evident.

Things went better after that. Over dinner they relaxed and talked. They covered the usual subjects—music, food, travel—but also some personal stuff. She discovered Kirk was an only child as she was. And he didn't care for Florida, to her surprise. His family had moved there only so he could play tennis year-round. He would have preferred to live in his hometown, St. Louis.

Shana liked listening to him, but more than that she enjoyed looking. He was *so* handsome! His style was a bit preppie for her taste, perhaps—he was wearing a knit tie and blue blazer— but that didn't matter. She loved the way his blue eyes flashed and the endearing way he smiled. He started with a shy grin and only gradually worked his way up to the real thing. By the time their dessert came, she was feeling a warm glow that grew whenever he smiled at her.

After dessert they split the check and left. Outside, Shana ran to the curb and flung up her arm for a taxi.

"Where to now, Miss Tour Guide?" Kirk said, flashing one of his slow grins. "The Empire State Building? The Statue of Liberty?"

Shana giggled. "Oh, you don't want to go to *those* places."

"I don't?" His smile faded a little.

"They're so touristy! What you want is to see the real New York—the places kids our age go to blow off steam."

"Okay—whatever you say," he agreed.

Because it was too early for Outer Space, they first toured some of her other favorite spots. At Tower Records near Lincoln Center, Kirk browsed happily for half an hour. Then Shana took him farther uptown to Mythology, a funky toy store on Columbus Avenue, to laugh at the weird gadgets. The next stop was a Mrs. Field's cookie store, where Kirk sampled every variety.

"I thought I ran hard on the tennis court!" he said to Shana finally. "How do you keep up this pace?"

Smiling, she brushed a crumb off his blazer. "Hey, we're barely getting started."

A minute later they were in yet another taxi, heading downtown. Shana was excited. It was the stop she had been waiting for—a club so fabulous it was sure to blow his socks off. She couldn't wait to see his face.

"Where are we now?" he asked, looking around in puzzlement at the dark, deserted street where the taxi had let them off.

"In the center of the universe," she said, giggling and leading him forward around a corner.

Just ahead was a roped-off entryway. Around it stood scores of people who hoped to be selected to go in. Pushing them aside, Shana blazed a trail up to the doorman.

"Hi," she said.

Without a word, the man pulled aside the velvet rope. As they went in, the crowd behind them groaned enviously.

Outer Space was hopping that night. The music was intense and the dance floor was jammed. Shana glanced around in satisfaction. The club had only been open for two months, but already it felt like a second home.

Kirk blinked as his eyes adjusted to the dimness. "Huh, it looks like a space station," he remarked when he could see.

Proudly Shana pointed out its features, from the aliens peering through portholes in the walls, to the enormous spiral-arm galaxy that spun slowly over the dance floor. She loved all the outer space touches, but even more she loved the mood that was fun and strictly down to earth.

"Want to dance?" she asked him eagerly.

He shrugged. "Since we're here—why not?"

Taking his large hand in her small one, she led him to the dance floor. In no time they were whirling and twisting, moving to the irresistible beat of the music.

Kirk was a good dancer, Shana noticed. He had an easy, fluid style that suited his tall, muscular frame. Her own style was more aggressive—a bit like a cyclone cutting loose, someone had once told her. Between them they attracted a good deal of attention, and she smiled, secretly satisfied. Dancing with Kirk was definitely heaven.

On and on they danced, sometimes moving in harmony, sometimes not. Shana was having the time of her life. She assumed Kirk was, too, until suddenly she caught him stifling a yawn.

"Hey, what's wrong?" she asked him, suppressing a rising sense of panic.

He smiled sheepishly. "Sorry, I guess I'm not used to staying up so late."

Is he serious? she wondered. He can't be! It's barely one o'clock.

"You don't want to leave, do you?"

"I, uh—" For a moment he looked ready to confirm her fears, but then his expression softened. "No, of course not."

She relaxed. "Whew! For a second there I thought you weren't having a good time!"

"I am—as long as you are too," he assured her.

They danced some more, but gradually Shana began to suspect that he was merely being polite. A glazed look was beginning to cloud his eyes, and his movements were becoming heavy.

Is it really Kirk's training routine that's making him look so out of it? Shana wondered. It has to be, she told herself. Believing that, she was about to say they should leave right that second so he could get some rest.

Then another thought stopped her from saying anything. It's me! I'm boring him! Kirk's in such great shape, I know he could party all night if he really wanted to!

She tried dancing up close to him, moving her body in a very sexy way. It had no effect. His movements were as wooden as before.

"Hey, let's go into the Launching Pad and get a Coke," she said. She pulled him off the dance floor and into the bar and began to chat. But even her funniest stories failed to rouse him. His eyes grew heavier by the minute.

Shana was panic-stricken. First Mitch—now Kirk! What am I doing wrong? she wondered.

Lifting his hand from his glass, she set it on the bar. "Let's go," she said.

After the noise of the club, the silence of the hallway in his hotel was a shock. Shana felt as if she had entered a tomb.

"You don't have to bring me all the way to my room," said Kirk, walking beside her.

Shana smiled nervously. Did that mean he wanted her to leave? "It comes with the tour—door-to-door service, you might say."

Kirk said nothing, and her nervousness increased. Maybe this wasn't such a good idea after all, she thought. Maybe I should just leave.

But, no—I can't give up that easily! she decided. Kirk is the nicest guy I've met in years. I can't let him go without making one more try.

At his door Shana took his key from his hand and turned it in the lock. When the door swung open, she marched inside.

"Um—Shana, is this part of the tour too?" he asked, shutting the door behind him.

"No, silly." She giggled too loudly. "I—I'd just like to use your bathroom, okay?"

"Sure."

Crossing the room, Shana caught a quick glance of twin beds, open suitcases, and a bag of racquets on the floor. Then she was in the bathroom, shutting the door behind her, her heart pounding. She didn't know which worried her more—the possibility that her plan would fail, or the possibility that it would succeed.

The plan, of course, was to perk up his interest with a little kissing. With most boys it usually worked, but with Kirk she wasn't so confident. He was so smart and self-assured! And he might not even like me, she thought.

A minute later she gave herself a final check in the mirror. Does my hair always look this wild after dancing? she wondered. Then, crossing her fingers for luck, she reentered his room.

"Kirk?"

At first she didn't see him. Maybe he went down the hall for some ice, she thought. But then her spirits sank. A figure lay on the couch, and coming from it was a sound that told her she had failed totally.

The sound was the soft, soul-destroying rumble of Kirk's snoring.

★

Six

"Shana, come here!"

Cursing under her breath, Shana turned to face her grandmother. She didn't feel like facing anyone at work that morning, least of all Edith. It was the day after the big disaster with Kirk, and she wanted only to die.

But probably even death wouldn't help me escape from Edith, she thought wryly. Sighing, she walked back up the dressing room corridor to where the Queen of the Soaps was standing.

"Yes, Grandma?"

Edith held out a photocopied sheet. "Here is a schedule of the rehearsals we'll have at home next week. Read it."

Shana tried, but the list of dates and scenes swam together in a blur. How did her grandmother expect her to focus after a night without sleep?

"Is everything clear?"

"Oh, sure."

"Good, then I shall expect you to be on time for each one."

"Can I go now?"

"Yes."

Turning, Shana went back up the corridor and turned into the studio. The second she was out of Edith's sight, she folded the schedule, crammed it into her back pocket, and forgot it.

Katie was involved in a dry-blocking rehearsal. As soon as she was finished, she came bounding over to greet her friend. "So, how'd it go?"

Shana's black expression said it all. "How do you think?"

"That bad, huh?"

"Worse."

Quickly Shana filled her in on all the details. It was an embarrassing story, but she held nothing back.

Katie looked puzzled when she had finished. "It sounds to me like he was telling the truth. I'll bet he always goes to bed early."

"But, Katie, it was only one o'clock! The sun had barely gone down!"

"Shana," Katie said, laughing, "I know we're on daylight savings time, but sunset is a lot earlier than that."

"Yeah, well, so what? I blew it anyway."

Together they walked down the middle of the studio. Around them, technicians were adjusting lights, rigging sound equipment, and moving props into position. It was just another hectic day at work for everyone else, but to Shana it felt like the end of the world. Why was she such a freak?

"Listen," Katie said. "I think that Kirk probably liked you a lot. It just sounds like his schedule's a lot different from yours."

"Who doesn't have time to have fun?" Shana objected. An image of Kirk asleep on his couch flashed through her mind.

"Nobody. But dancing till dawn wouldn't turn on a morning person like him."

"What are you saying?"

"My point is, next time you should plan a date that involves things *Kirk* likes to do. He has some interests outside tennis, doesn't he?"

"Well . . ." Shana toyed with a button on her blouse. Why hadn't *she* thought of that?

"Another thing," Katie went on. "Next time I think your date with him should be during the day. Give the poor guy a chance to appreciate you!"

"Yeah, right. Great idea. Thanks a lot," Shana said glumly.

The problem was, she doubted there would even *be* a next time. For one thing, when would they set it up? Kirk wouldn't be appearing on the show again, and she certainly wasn't going to run into him on a tennis court! No, the only hope was that he would call her, and that, she knew, was about as likely as a snowstorm. What guy in his right mind would want to be bored into a stupor twice?

Reaching the back wall of the barnlike studio, they turned and headed back. Seeing her friend's forlorn expression, Katie decided it was time to change the subject.

"Well, how're things going with your grandmother?" she asked.

"Don't ask!"

Katie reddened. "Sorry. I was only trying to help."

"I know. But Grandma's driving me nuts too." All at once she remembered the schedule in her back pocket. Taking it out, she handed it to Katie. "Here, look at this. Grandma expects me to rehearse harder at home than here."

"Wow!" Katie's eyes bugged out. "She's got you booked every night next week."

"Galley slaves in ancient Rome had it easier than me."

"Well, look on the bright side," Katie said. "How many times in your life will you get to learn from an actress as terrific as she is?"

"Too many."

"I'm serious! Everyone in the cast thinks she's brilliant, Shana."

It was true. In the week and a half since Edith had started, Shana had heard nothing but praise for her grandmother. At times Shana thought that if another person told her how wonderful or divine or talented her grandmother was, she'd be sick.

She clenched her teeth. "I don't care whether she's brilliant or not. I don't want to spend every evening doing exactly what I do all day. Somehow I'm going to find a way to kill that plot line, Katie. I swear it!"

Just then Mitch approached them. Shana felt her stomach plummet. It had been rough working with Mitch since their breakup. Off the set, at least, she had managed to avoid him, but right then there was no escape.

It was Katie he wanted though. "Clayton wants to reblock the scene we just did," he announced.

"Okay, I'll be right there." Turning, Katie took her hand and squeezed it. "Cheer up, okay? I'm sure things will work out."

"Thanks."

Then Katie was gone, dashing back to her scene. Mitch lingered a moment. "Shana, I—"

"Forget it," she said, narrowing her eyes. "I don't want to hear it."

Brushing past him, she headed for the outer door. The last thing I need, she told herself, is to probe old wounds—especially since the ones I inflicted on myself last night are still fresh.

Yes, it was much better to look to the future. Too bad the future looked so grim!

The morning dragged on. Finally Clayton called a lunch break. Instantly Shana sped to her dressing room to change. She had an hour, and she wanted to use every minute.

As she headed out the front door of the studio, she glanced right and left, wondering which way to go. Half of her wanted to eat, and half of her wanted to take a long, slow walk in Central Park. Before she could make up her mind, she heard someone call her name.

"Shana?" A stretch limousine was sitting at the curb in front of the studio. And leaning out of a side door was Kirk!

"I don't believe it!"

Embarrassment and joy flooded through her. She felt as though she had walked out of a nightmare into a fantasy.

"Shana, can we talk?" Kirk asked, stepping onto the sidewalk.

"Sure, where?"

He gestured into the limousine's backseat. "How about right here?"

It took her exactly one second to make up her mind. She jumped inside and sank down into the rich, creamy leather upholstery.

Only after Kirk had joined her and pulled the door closed did she notice the cellophane-wrapped roses sitting on the seat.

"Kirk! Are those for—"

"That's right," he said, looking down at his feet. "They're for you. I want to apologize for falling asleep on you last night. You must think I'm a real jerk."

Suddenly there was a lump in her throat and a hot stinging behind her eyes. "I-I don't think you're a jerk at all," she told him. "The whole thing was really my fault."

"No. It was mine. I was really a rude, stupid idiot."

"But you wouldn't have fallen asleep if I hadn't bored you!"

"Bored me?" he echoed in disbelief. "Shana, you must be kidding. Last night—well, let's just say there were times when I thought I was on a date with a hurricane. You blew me away!"

"I *did*?"

He smiled shyly. "Yeah, you did."

Relief swept through her. It's like a dream, she thought—a great, big, beautiful dream! He *likes* me—and I like him too.

Impulsively, she threw her arms around his neck. They hugged for a moment before she settled back with a laugh. "Whew. You just made me the happiest girl in New York."

"I'd like to go out with you again, and this time I promise to have a cup of coffee beforehand."

Shana laughed. "I have a better idea. This time, why don't we get together during the day?" She sent a mental thank-you to Katie.

"Sounds good, but don't you have to work?"

"During the week. Not on Saturday, though."

"Saturday is great," he confirmed. "What would you like to do?"

Wracking her brain, Shana struggled to come up with a suggestion. She didn't want to do any of the things they had done on their first date—that would be bad luck.

Suddenly inspiration hit. "How about a game of tennis? We can get a court in Central Park."

He smiled. "Sure you want to play me?"

"Don't worry, I can handle it," she answered. "The question is, can *you*?"

Kirk threw back his head and laughed. "Normally I'd say yes, but now I don't know. If you move around the court as fast as you moved last night, I may be in big trouble!"

Shana laughed too. She had never felt so good in her life, she decided. She never wanted to go back to the studio. On the other hand, though, she didn't want to push her luck.

"Well, I'll see you Saturday," she said, moving toward the door.

"Shana, wait. I have a little time right now—"

"I'm on my lunch hour—"

"What were you going to do?" he asked.

Shana picked up the roses he had bought her. They were beautiful, twelve perfect stems. "I *was* going to walk in the park—"

"Want to drive instead?"

Her smile was all he needed to see. Leaning forward, he tapped on the glass that separated them from the limo's driver.

The partition slid open. "Yes, sir?" the driver asked.

"Would you drive through the park, please?" Kirk requested. "Oh, and Max?"

"Yes, sir?"

Kirk grinned. "Take it slow."

There was only an hour or so of daylight left that night as Shana and Katie arrived at the Central Park tennis courts. Final taping had run late, and then they had to stop at Katie's apartment so Katie could change into shorts and grab a pair of racquets.

Shana was nervous. "Are you sure we'll get a court?"

"Relax," Katie said. "I already told you that my dad had already reserved it. All we have to do is sign in at the fieldhouse."

Reaching the end of the path, Katie tossed down the pink nylon duffle bag that held their equipment. She sat on a bench and began to unlace her running shoes.

"You're lucky, you know," Katie remarked as she slipped on her white tennis sneakers. "If you hadn't worn shorts and sneakers to work today, we wouldn't be able to do this."

Shana nodded. "I know. There wouldn't have been enough time for me to go home. We're lucky your folks lent us the court too."

"What else could they do? This is an emergency!"

A minute later they signed in and made their way onto the court. Shana was amazed at the size of the facility. Twenty or thirty courts were spread out over an area as large as a football field.

Katie snapped open a vacuum-sealed can of tennis balls. "I still don't believe you, Shana," she said. "It took some nerve to challenge Kirk to a tennis game."

"You were the one who suggested we do something *he* enjoys!" Shana pointed out.

"True, but I never thought you'd come up with tennis. You don't even know how to play!"

Shana looked around. In the court next to them a white-haired couple was lobbing a ball back and forth across the net. It didn't look too difficult.

She picked up a racquet. "Well, I may not know how to play yet, but I'm sure you can teach me," she said confidently.

Shaking her head, Katie led her onto the court for a lesson. They faced each other across the net.

"Hey! Don't look so worried!" Shana called over. "Just serve to me."

"Now? With no practice or anything?"

Shana nodded confidently.

The first ball zipped by her, and she tripped over her racket trying to get it. The next ball hit her in the knee.

"Hey, wait a minute!" she called to Katie.

"Wait a minute, *what*? You want to learn to play, don't you?"

"Sure," Shana grumbled. "But I'd like to be alive while I'm doing it! Come on—serve to me again."

Seven

The next morning Shana waited anxiously for an opportunity to slip away from the studio. It seemed she wouldn't get one, but then Edith was called to have her hair set. Perfect, she thought. I'll have half an hour to myself.

She had finally worked up the courage to talk to Sally Conners about the Jasmin-Betty plot line. She was taking a big risk, she knew. The story line was creating good publicity for "All That Glitters." Two Bradburys were working together for the first time in decades; in the last week, articles pointing out that fact had appeared in the entertainment trade papers. Even *People* had been calling for an interview. According to the network publicity department, she and Edith could be on its cover. But Shana hoped she was important enough to the show that Sally would take her feelings into account. Working with her grandmother was making her a nervous wreck.

Thank goodness for Kirk, she thought. Knowing he liked her gave her the confidence she needed to face Sally.

In no time she was out the front door of the studio and across the street, where the building that housed the soap's executive offices was located.

In Sally Conners's outer office, her executive assistant, stone-faced Brenda Vogel, regarded her with cool disdain.

"May I tell Sally *why* you wish to see her?" the woman asked once Shana had explained what she wanted. Her eyebrows twitched.

"It's personal," Shana said, dodging. "But please tell her it's *important*." She put on a worried look for emphasis.

"Very well." Rising, Brenda tapped on Sally's door, then disappeared inside.

Brenda probably thinks I'm in some kind of trouble, Shana thought, but that doesn't matter. The important thing right now is getting in to see Sally.

A moment later she was shown in. Sally was a slim, well-dressed woman in her fifties. She had a manner that could be very sharp. Known as a no-nonsense producer, she demanded the best from her cast and crew, and she generally got it.

"So," Sally said, when they had settled down on opposite sides of her desk, "what's this personal problem that's got you upset?"

Briefly Shana stated her position. "I don't like the Jasmin-Betty plot line. I don't think I'm doing my best work in it. I know it can't be changed right away, but could the writers work it back toward the way it was?"

Sally leaned back, clearly surprised. "Shana, you know we can't change our plot to satisfy the whims of the cast."

"Sometimes you can," Shana pointed out. "My grandmother made a suggestion, and wham! The next week we were doing scenes together."

"I'm afraid it wasn't as simple as that," Sally said, toying with a pencil. "In reality, the plot was suggested by your grandmother quite awhile ago. Indeed, it was one of her conditions for appearing on our show."

"What!"

"It's true. At first I was reluctant to agree to it, I don't mind telling you. I didn't feel your acting skills were up to the job."

Shana was stunned. "Y-you didn't?"

"No. But then your grandmother assured me that your performance would improve, so I went along with the idea," she explained.

Shana couldn't believe what she was hearing. Edith's actions had been even more deliberate than she thought! And worse, Sally felt that her acting was weak. Why hadn't she ever mentioned it before?

Sally smiled. "If you're worrying about what I said a second ago, don't. In the last week your acting has made a big improvement. I think it has been your best work so far."

"Thanks." She was a little relieved, but not much.

"Working with your grandmother seems to have been good for you."

"So you wouldn't consider changing the plot?"

There was a short pause. Sally was obviously annoyed, but at the same time she wanted to handle the situation tactfully. She toyed with her pencil some more.

"I'm afraid the answer is no, Shana," she said at last. "The story line has too many things going for it."

Shana's heart sank. "Such as?"

"Well, for one thing, the publicity has been phenomenal. I don't have to tell you that."

Shana looked down.

"There's another thing, too," Sally added. "The story itself is dynamite. In just the past three days when the new story has aired, our viewers are crazy about it. They're lapping it up."

Shana could understand that too. It was a clever plot. It had a sympathetic central character in Betty, a woman who had arrived in Fairhope without any memory. There was a mystery—who was trying to kill her?—and even a touch of the supernatural, thanks to Jasmin. All those were elements that soap audiences loved.

But there was one thing Sally wasn't saying: Edith and the Bradbury legacy were more important to the show than Shana herself. Once again, her grandmother had out-ranked her. Miserable, Shana collapsed in her chair.

"I'm sorry, Shana," Sally said quietly.

The sun was streaming through the vertical slats of Sally's drawn blinds. The pattern it cast on the carpet reminded Shana of prison bars. Am I ever going to escape from Edith's ambition? she wondered.

"There's one thing I don't understand," she said doggedly. "Why did my grandmother go on this kick to improve my acting?"

"I think she wants to help you."

"No, I mean what set her off? What started her thinking about me?"

The producer frowned. "You know, it's funny. When I asked her what had convinced her to come over to our show, she said there was one particular episode that had spurred her to work with you."

"Which one?"

"Katie Nolan's premiere."

Once again Shana picked up on Sally's unspoken words: the quality of Katie's acting had obviously made Edith realize that Shana needed some help.

As she rode down in the elevator, Shana was trembling, whether from rage or from humiliation she couldn't tell. It wasn't Katie's fault, she knew, but still she couldn't help feeling angry. If Katie weren't such a brilliant actress, then her grandmother might never have joined "Glitters." Things would be the way they had been before.

I'm not such a bad actress, she thought defensively. It's just Sally who thinks so. Then, just as she was approaching the studio entrance, she stopped short. Yes, she thought. I *can* act. . . .

Her body tensed, Shana waited for the explosion. One—two—three—four—fi—

"Cuuuut! Jasmin, where are you? You just missed your cue!"

Clayton Tyler's voice sounded irritated as it came over the control booth speaker. It was the middle of dress rehearsal—not a good time, she knew, for her to blow an entrance. Pushing open the prop door, she burst onto the set.

"Oh—I'm s-sorry," she stammered, feigning embarrassment.

"Wake up, Shana," Clayton's voice said. "Let's take it from the top."

As the floor manager waved the cameras and boom mikes back into position, Shana suppressed a smile. She was especially pleased by the annoyed look on her grandmother's face. Overall, she decided, phase one of her plan was an unqualified success. Now for phase two . . .

They started again. The scene they were rehearsing was one between Betty and Jasmin. In it, Betty would receive a phone call warning her to get out of Fairhope. Then Jasmin—who was using her psychic powers to help Betty discover her true identity—would come in and console her. It was a simple scene. Easy to do—normally.

"Who is this, please? Won't you tell me . . . oh, no!"

Shana recognized Betty's line. It signaled that the anonymous caller had hung up, and it was her entrance cue. That time she opened the door on cue.

"Hello, Betty. I have good news for you. I found out—oh, what ees wrong?"

She played the role of Jasmin in a lightly accented voice. The ease with which she spoke came from practice. Unlike stage acting, TV acting had to be very natural. Big gestures and quick movements did not work; emotion was conveyed through facial expression.

The scene went smoothly up to the point when Jasmin was supposed to assure Betty that she would get her memory back soon. Suddenly Shana "forgot" her line.

"Betty, you must not—must not—oh, rats! What do I say now?" Her accent dropped away as she resumed her normal voice.

The scene was ruined.

"Cuuut! Shana, would you come over to the control booth, please?"

Shana's heart was pounding as she made her way across the studio floor. So far phase two was working beautifully, but what would happen next? Would Clayton, the key to her scheme, play into her hands? Would he chew her out?

Clayton stepped out of the control booth. He was a polished-looking man with an angular face and curly hair streaked with silver. As a director he was efficient—a necessity in soaps—but Shana didn't like him. He had a reputation as a letch, and had once tried to come on to Katie.

His other problem was that he angered easily, but now she hoped to use his quick temper to her advantage. Her heart leapt when she saw the look on his face. He was fuming!

"What's going on, Shana?" he snapped. "Don't you know we're in dress rehearsal? We tape this scene in less than an hour!"

"I know. I'm s-sorry," she said, making her lower lip tremble.

He didn't realize she was acting. "Forget the waterworks. Just tell me why you're having trouble with this scene *now*. You played it perfectly this morning, I noticed."

This was exactly the opening Shana was hoping for. "It's my grandmother," she said, faking a nervous swallow.

"She makes you edgy?"

"That's putting it mildly!" she groaned. "When we do a scene together, I get so rattled I can hardly think straight."

"Hmm—"

Shana held her breath as Clayton studied her through narrowed eyes. Was he thinking what she hoped he was thinking?

Once Clayton had grown so disgusted with the offstage hysterics between Mitch and Katie that he had actually cancelled a scene—right in the middle of the day! A substitute scene had had to be mounted quickly, at great expense to the show.

She didn't expect him to cancel the Jasmin-Betty scene—it was too close to taping for that—but if she *could* convince him that she couldn't work with Edith, then maybe—just maybe—he would go to Sally and request a change in the story. Edith would still be on the show, of course, but at least they wouldn't have to work together so much.

Clay grunted. "I don't get it. You've been living with her your whole life, and only now she's getting under your skin?"

"Clay!" she wailed. "Living with her and working with her are two—"

Suddenly he pointed a finger in her face. "Okay, listen up. I'll forget about your screw-ups a minute ago. Just be sure you don't flub it during taping. If you do, there'll be trouble." With that, he stormed back inside the control booth.

Trouble, huh? Shana thought. That's just what I'm looking for!

As usual the studio was dead quiet during taping. Waiting for her cue behind the prop door, Shana imagined she could hear her own heart beating. Phase three of her plan was about to go into effect, and she was edgy.

"Who is this, please? Won't you tell me . . . oh, no!"

As her cue line arrived, it took every ounce of willpower she had not to open the door. Messing up went against her instincts. Slowly she counted. One—two—three—

The explosion never came. Instead, there was only an expectant hush. Unable to bear the tension any longer, she pushed the door open. On the set Edith, as Betty, was pacing back and forth as if searching for something she had mislaid.

She's acting as if the silence was part of the script! Shana realized.

"Hello, Betty. I have good news for you. I found out—oh, what ees wrong?"

Shana slipped into her dialogue, wondering what to do. Phase three was a bust, unless—suddenly another option occurred to her.

When they reached the point where Jasmin was to comfort Betty, she again "forgot" her line. "Betty, you must not—must not—"

"Give up hope?" Betty supplied, smiling weakly. "Oh, I know. I'll get my memory back just as surely as your English will improve!"

Shana reddened. Edith had ad-libbed beautifully, using Jasmin's own line to cover the error. Wasn't there *any* hope of ruining the scene?

Gradually the scene's conclusion approached. Jasmin was supposed to offer to consult the police about the crank call, then run out the door. A final, desperate possibility came to her.

When her cue came, she took a deep breath and turned. Instead of running for the door, however, she ran straight into a small prop table. The bric-a-brac on its top spilled to the floor with a loud clatter.

Edith didn't miss a beat. "Oh, my goodness—there they are!" Reaching into the clutter, she picked up a pair of bifocals. "I've been looking for my glasses all day. Thank you, dear— you truly are psychic!"

That did it! Crushed, Shana realized that there was no way to fight it. Edith's professionalism would cover any mistake.

After the scene, Clayton approached them. "Nice scene, you two. It was very smooth. You make a great team."

As he said it, he eyed Shana sarcastically. A hot flush of embarrassment spread through her entire body. So much for phase three! she thought. Her plan was a washout.

Later, as she and her grandmother rode home together, Shana cringed. Outside it was sweltering, but in the back of the cab the temperature was chilly. Edith was not amused.

"I am deeply—*deeply* disappointed in you, Shana," she said, glaring. "I thought you were making progress, but now I see we'll have to work harder. Please be ready for an extra-long rehearsal tonight."

Slowly, Shana slid down in her seat. Now she had really done it. Thanks to her brilliant plan, her predicament was worse than ever. At least I have one thing to look forward to, she consoled herself. On Saturday she would see Kirk!

★

Eight

As she stepped from the taxi at Central Park West, Shana glanced up in concern. The sky overhead was dark. Angry gray clouds were rushing by. A storm was threatening. It would be a godsend if her tennis game with Kirk were rained out. He was going to annihilate her!

How did I get myself into this mess? she wondered. What made me open my big, fat mouth? True, she had managed to lob a few balls back to Katie during their lesson. But she had played one game, and he was a pro! It was ridiculous.

Kirk was waiting at the fieldhouse, his equipment bag in his hand. Other players were looking at him out of the corners of their eyes. In spite of her nervousness, Shana smiled when she saw him. He looked fantastic in his white shorts and warm-up jacket.

"Hi! All set for the big challenge?" he asked as she approached.

"You bet," she said, lying. "I'm going to wipe the court with you!"

He laughed. "All right! That's the spirit. John McEnroe, watch out!"

Shana smiled tightly. Who is this McEnroe guy, anyway? she wondered.

She signed in. As Kirk was paying for the court that she had reserved in advance, the man behind the counter stared. He seemed to recognize Kirk, but then he shook his head. "Nah— you couldn't be. For a sec I thought you were Kirk Tucker!"

"A lot of people make that mistake." Kirk nodded, his face perfectly straight.

Shana giggled as they made their way to their court. "Why didn't you tell him who you were?" she wanted to know.

"And have everybody asking for my autograph? No thank you. I'd rather spend my time with you."

Her knees went weak.

When they reached their court, Kirk unzipped his racquet. While he did, Shana bent over and tried to touch her toes. What should I do? she asked herself. If I go through with this I'll look like an idiot, but if I tell him the truth I'll look like an idiot too.

Straightening, she decided there was only one logical thing she could do: play him. Who could tell? Maybe a miracle would happen.

"Would you like to warm up first?" Kirk asked from across the court. He was rapidly bouncing a ball with his racquet.

Show off, she thought. "Who needs to warm up? Let's just play."

"Sure thing, but—uh, wouldn't you like to stand a little farther back?"

Shana checked her position. Hadn't Katie said the middle of the court was the best spot? She couldn't remember. "No thanks. I'll stay where I am."

"Suit yourself."

Kirk tossed a ball high in the air. Then, in a motion so sudden and powerful that Shana barely saw it, he sprang from the ground and snapped his racquet. A *whooock!* filled the air. The ball whizzed by her at the speed of light.

"Uh, Kirk . . ." she began.

He smiled. "A little fast for you? Tell you what, why don't I play at half speed?"

Why don't you tie your legs together? she thought. "Maybe you'd better."

"You got it."

Taking a second ball from the pocket of his shorts, Kirk tossed it in the air. *Whooock!* That time she actually saw it, but before she could get her legs in gear, the ball had bounced into the chain link fence behind her.

He served a third time. *Whooock!* Shana jabbed her racquet out, but missed the ball by several feet. *Surely the game has to be over by now,* she thought. *This is ruthless slaughter!*

Kirk was bouncing the ball at his baseline, getting ready to serve again, when suddenly a booming clap of thunder shook the city. A drop of rain fell nearby—then another—and another. In no time they were caught in a downpour.

"Uh-oh," Kirk shouted. "There goes our game!"

"Darn! Just when I was getting warmed up!" she groaned.

Quickly they grabbed their gear and headed for the fieldhouse. When they arrived, however, they found it jammed with players who had reached it before them. They couldn't get inside.

"Quick! What should we do?" Kirk asked her. He had his warm-up jacket pulled over his head.

"Run for it!" she cried, taking off.

Hand in hand, they ran up the path toward Central Park West. Kirk's equipment bag slapped against his legs. Shana tried to cover her head with her racquet, but it was no help. She had left its cover behind. She was getting soaked.

Suddenly it all became too much—the trees waving in the wind—the rain coming down in sheets—the two of them running hand in hand.

She began to laugh. Kirk started in, too, and that made Shana laugh even harder.

By the time they reached Central Park West, she was shrieking. Kirk was howling wildly. Together they sprinted down Central Park West and then turned on a side street, heading for fashionable Columbus Avenue. When they reached it, they stood on the corner, looking around. They were still holding hands, Shana realized. She felt wonderful.

"What do we do now?" Kirk gasped. His hair was plastered to his head, and water was running down his neck.

"Look for someplace dry!" she said, realizing she probably looked worse.

A second later they spotted a sidewalk café. They ran for it, ducked under its awning, and collapsed at a table.

"Whew! You look like you just swam the English Channel," he said.

"Oh, yeah? Well, you look like a sponge!" she replied.

"May I take your order?" a waiter asked. He looked totally unsurprised to find them there, dripping water on the sidewalk.

A short while later they were sipping hot cappuccino. Shana leaned over her mug, inhaling the lovely coffee and cinnamon steam. She had dried off and combed her hair in the ladies' room, so she felt almost civilized again. What a day!

Kirk had combed his hair back too. Normally he had wavy golden blond hair, but now his hair was darker looking and straight. He looks like a tall, blue-eyed Rudolph Valentino, Shana thought—very suave and terribly dashing.

She looked up from her mug. "Kirk, I have a confession to make."

"Oh?"

"I don't really know how to play tennis."

"I know you don't," Kirk told her. "I figured that out a long time ago."

Shana smothered another round of giggles. "You did?"

Kirk grinned. "Yeah," he said. "Most people only want to talk about tennis when they meet me. But not you. When you walked into that dressing room—and later, when we went out— you talked about anything *but* tennis. That's what tipped me off—that and, today, you didn't care that your racquet was getting soaked."

Shana looked at him coyly. "Then are you sorry you agreed to have a game with me?"

Kirk's eyes went soft. "Isn't it obvious that I wanted to see you again?"

"But you could have suggested something else. I mean, why let me make a fool of myself?"

He sipped his cappuccino. "Who says you looked like a fool? Going out on that court with me took a lot of guts."

"Either that or a lot of stupidity." In spite of her words she was smiling.

The rain continued for several hours. They sat at their cozy table and talked. This time there was nothing superficial about their conversation. Shana discovered they had a lot in common.

"I know exactly what you mean," Kirk said after she had explained the hard time she was having with her grandmother. "My dad is just like that. He's been pushing me to play tennis since I was six years old. I know he means well, but sometimes I think my career means more to him than it does to me. I mean, when I win he's on top of the world. When I lose, he pushes me harder."

"You enjoy playing tennis, though, don't you?" she asked, thinking about her own mixed feelings about acting.

"Oh, sure. It's a lot of fun. Or it was . . ." His voice trailed off.

"Was?"

He stirred his spoon around his empty cup. "The thing is, I liked it when I was doing the junior tour. You know, tournaments for kids eighteen and under? I got to hang out with guys my own age, and some of them were close friends."

"And now?"

"Now I'm on the pro tour, and that's different. There's more pressure, and the people aren't so friendly. Guys like Jimmy Connors are okay, but they're *old*! We don't relate to each other very well, you know what I mean?"

Shana nodded. She sure did. It had always been a drag being a kid actor in the theater. Working on "Glitters" wasn't so bad because there were so many teens on the show.

"Kirk, do you ever think about what you'll do when you stop playing tennis—as a pro, I mean?" she asked him.

"Sure, all the time. I haven't reached any conclusions yet though. I figure I don't have to decide anything now. I'm only eighteen."

Shana knew how he felt—sometimes she couldn't bear to think about her future. There were other times, though, when she felt she ought to have it all planned out. If she didn't, she worried, she might wind up drifting through life aimlessly, without goals, or worse, with shallow ones.

The rain continued. It was cool outside the café, but inside herself Shana was gradually becoming aware of warm, new feelings. She had never felt so comfortable—so *connected*—with a boy before. And when she looked into Kirk's gorgeous blue eyes her heart began to pound and a fluttery sensation turned her stomach in circles.

After a while, Kirk took a deep breath and looked her squarely in the eye. "Shana, there's something I want to ask you."

She tensed. "Yes?"

"Are you—I mean, do you—ah—oh, why can't I just ask it? Do you have a boyfriend?" he blurted out.

Shana laughed. "Of course not." Why had *that* been so hard to ask? "Do you really think I'd be out with you if I did?"

He looked embarrassed. "No! But I had to know for sure."

"To tell you the truth, I did have a boyfriend up until about two weeks ago," she said.

"It was that guy on 'All That Glitters,' wasn't it?" he asked, suddenly turning cool. "The one who plays Matt—"

Shana was flabbergasted. "How did you know that?"

Kirk held up his hand and sneezed. "I just had a feeling. The minute I saw him on the show, I—"

"You've been watching 'Glitters'?" Shana asked in surprise.

"Yeah, to see you." Kirk sniffled and blew his nose. "Anyway, the minute I saw him I just knew, somehow, that he's the type of guy who'd go after you. He strikes me as being pretty intense."

"He is. *Too* intense."

Kirk had been watching "Glitters"—just to see *her*!

"Shana, I . . ." He paused, looking down helplessly at his hands. Shana sensed that he was about to say something important.

"Shana, would you—hey, look! The sun is coming out!"

Quickly she snapped her head around. It was true! Up and down Columbus Avenue, bright shafts of sunlight were streaming down, picking out buildings, even whole blocks, like giant follow spots aimed on a stage. Suddenly the sunlight hit their café, bathing them in a bright, warm glare.

Shana felt a smile break across her face. "All *right*! Let's go!" she said.

They paid their bill, gathered up their gear, and headed back toward Central Park.

Slowly they made their way past Belvedere Castle and into the Ramble.

"You sure you can get us out of here?" Kirk asked as they walked through the maze of paths. He sneezed loudly again.

"Just stick with me, kid," Shana answered, handing him a tissue from her bag. Walking so close to him, she felt as if she were flying.

When they came to the wrought-iron bridge that spanned the narrow part of The Lake, they paused to watch the empty rowboats rocking in the ripples of the water. Setting his equipment bag down, Kirk turned to Shana. Then he took her gently in his arms and kissed her.

Shana felt pure, liquid pleasure flow through every inch of her. Kissing Kirk felt so good, so right! She melted against him and clung tightly.

Finally she drew her head back for air. "Kirk," she said in a soft voice. "What were you going to say in the restaurant—you know, just before the sun came out?"

Kirk smiled. "Just that I'm glad you barged into that dressing room."

"I'm glad too."

Then they were kissing again, and it was a long while before either of them came up for air. Shana was in heaven.

Suddenly Kirk staggered back—he couldn't stop sneezing.

"Kirk, are you—"

"Ah—choo!"

"You look pale," Shana said. "You're perspiring too." Gently she touched his forehead.

"I'm sorry, Shana," Kirk said apologetically, "but I don't feel so well. I've been fighting a cold for a few days, and I think the rain did me in."

Concerned, Shana scooped up his equipment bag, and linked his arm with hers.

"Kirk Tucker, you're going back to your hotel right now," she informed him. "You should get some rest."

"But—"

Shana shook her head. "No," she ordered. "No buts, Mr. Tennis Pro. *Sleep*."

★
Nine

As the taping ended on Monday, Shana was pleased. Her final scene had been with Edith, true, but it had been a scene she liked. In it, Jasmin used her psychic powers to try to help Betty Balfour discover her true identity. She tried to "read" Betty's aura.

What she discovered was that Betty had no aura. Jasmin raised the possibility that Betty was not human, but a ghost of someone from Fairhope's past, come to expose the guilty secrets of certain town residents.

Shana smiled as Clayton's voice came over the control booth speaker.

"Nice work, Jasmin. A very convincing scene!"

Clayton gave out compliments sparingly, she knew, and *never* broadcast them for the whole studio to hear. Turning, she began to walk away from the set. But then a sharp command stopped her.

"Shana, stay put. I want to remind you that we have a rehearsal at home this evening at eight o'clock sharp," Edith said.

Shana wheeled around. "I *know*. I'll be there." She had practically memorized the schedule her grandmother had given her the week before.

"See that you are. And whatever your 'errand' is—please be careful."

Earlier, Shana had informed her grandmother that she wouldn't be home for dinner that night; she had something important to do. Don't worry, I won't spoil your precious rehearsal by getting mugged, she thought. It was as if Edith cared about Shana only as an actress—another Bradbury to carry on the name.

For a fraction of a second she studied her grandmother. Done up as Betty Balfour in a simple print dress, her white hair pulled back in a bun, she was the picture of helpless innocence. How ironic!

Then Shana turned and dashed off to change and remove her makeup. Sprinting down the outer corridor, she swung through her dressing room door—and stopped dead. Sitting in her extra chair, crying miserably, was Katie.

"What's the matter?" she asked, concerned for her friend.

Katie wiped her eyes. "It's M-Mitch." She hiccuped. "He's a creep. When we were through taping our scene, he—he—" She couldn't finish. Fresh tears began to run down her cheeks.

Shana wrapped her arms protectively around Katie. That creep! she thought angrily. She was going to get him for hurting Katie.

"There, there—it's okay. Tell me all about it," she offered.

"Oh, Shana, it was awful," Katie explained. "Our scene didn't go well. When it was over, he said that I'd better shape up."

"*You?*" Shana couldn't believe her ears. Katie was probably the best actress on the show, except maybe for Edith. "I can't believe that guy. If anyone should shape up it's him. What else did he say?"

"That was it."

"It was?" Puzzled, she drew her eyebrows together. "Well, his tone was nasty, I'll bet. It had to be, if he upset you like this."

Katie shook her head. "He didn't shout or anything, if that's what you mean. He said it kind of quietly, you know?"

"And you started crying over *that*?"

"Shana, he hurt my feelings! Why is he so mean to me?" Wailing, she began to cry again. Tears streamed down her face.

Collapsing on her makeup stool, Shana plucked a tissue from its box and handed it to Katie. Frankly, she thought her friend was being oversensitive. If Mitch had done that to her, it would have rolled off her back like water.

Maybe Katie is too thin-skinned, she thought. Or maybe she just has to get used to the pressures of soap opera production. After all, she had only started eight weeks before. Still, there was something about Katie's reaction that bothered her. What was it?

Katie sniffed, her sobs coming to an end. "Sorry, Shana, I didn't mean to dump on you like that."

"That's what I'm here for, right?" she assured her. "I just think you're nuts for letting Mitch get to you. I mean, why worry about a guy who makes you cry when there are plenty of guys around who could make you smile?"

She was thinking about Kirk. Sunday on the phone with Katie, she had spent hours describing their Saturday together. Each moment sparkled in her memory like a diamond.

Katie reached over and squeezed her hand. "I'm so happy for you, Shana." She knew without asking what Shana was thinking about. "You deserve a terrific guy like Kirk."

"Thanks," she said, beaming. "Speaking of him, I've got to get going."

"You're meeting him tonight?" Katie asked, rising from her chair.

"He doesn't know it yet, but, yeah, I am."

"Shana? What are you planning?"

She grinned. "Nothing much. A mission of mercy, you might say."

When Katie had gone, she furiously began to smear cold cream on her face. Normally she would have taken more time to remove her makeup, but tonight she had to be home by eight. She wanted every extra minute she could get.

The elevator doors slid open with a *ding*. Shana stepped out and sped down the hotel corridor toward Kirk's room.

She rapped on his door. When he opened it, his jaw dropped. "I don't believe it. Shana!"

"It's Dr. Bradbury to you," she informed him, sweeping into his room. Looking around, she set down the shopping bag she was carrying. It was from Zabar's, the famous West Side delicatessen. "And how is the patient tonight? Getting better?"

"A little." Kirk smiled weakly as he closed the door.

He did look a little better, Shana noticed, but not much. He was still pale, but now his nose was red. His eyes were bloodshot too. She felt a rush of sympathy for him.

"What's in the bag?" he asked.

"Among other things, chicken soup . . ." Reaching down, she pulled out a plastic container. "And killer fudge." She giggled. "If the soup doesn't make you feel better, then you eat the fudge and die."

Kirk laughed. "You know, you're just what the doctor ordered."

Setting the soup on his desk, she flew into the waiting circle of his arms. She stayed there for a long time, hugging him, her head tucked in the hollow of his shoulder. She knew she was right where she belonged.

Finally, though, he coughed. She drew away. "Are you okay?"

"Sure. I went to see a doctor today, and he told me I'd be over this in a few days, maybe sooner. I hope it's sooner, though. The first round of the tournament is coming up."

Shana nodded. She had seen a newspaper ad for the charity event that morning. The lineup of tennis pros and celebrities was spectacular.

"Do you know who your doubles partner will be, yet?" she asked.

"Yes, she's that movie actress, Gloria Ziegler. Do you know her?"

"Slightly. We did a movie together when I was twelve." She relaxed. Gloria was about forty—no threat. She had worried that Kirk would be paired with some cute young thing.

"Oh, while I'm thinking of it . . ." Kirk rummaged in a drawer and handed her a small envelope. "A front row ticket to the final match."

"Wow! Thanks." She was overjoyed that he had thought of her, but she couldn't resist teasing him a little. "You think you and Gloria will make it that far?"

"Will you be there on Saturday?"

She nodded.

"Then I'll see to it that we make it."

Happiness flooded through her. She had no doubt he'd keep his word.

As Kirk ate his soup wih a plastic spoon, she walked around his room. It felt good to be there— even if it was only his temporary home. Then she noted the TV.

"Hey, did you catch your spot on 'Glitters' today?" she asked. The episode on which he had appeared had aired that afternoon.

"Yeah. Luckily it was short. You were really great, though, especially in that scene with your grandmother," he said, referring to the scene in which Jasmin first agreed to aid Betty.

"Thanks."

"I really mean it. I was impressed. I couldn't believe how much emotion you packed into just a couple of lines."

Gradually their conversation moved on to other topics. They talked about friends, the press. Kirk told her how he felt when he had won the French Open; she explained why she loved to perform Shakespeare.

"So," Kirk said, "is the beautiful Shakespearean actress looking forward to going back to school this fall?"

Shana shrugged. "I don't think I'll mind."

Kirk rolled his eyes. "That's because you lucked out. You go to that Professional—what's it called?"

"The Professional Children's School." Shana propped herself up on one elbow. "The schedule there is pretty loose."

Kirk grinned. "I guess you don't mind that."

"You bet I don't. I don't need to be a slave at home and at school too!"

By this time they were on opposite ends of his bed: he reclining at its head, she lying at its foot.

"Shana, what does your mom think about your acting? Can't she help you get your grandmother off your case?" Kirk asked.

"I hardly know her," Shana answered honestly. "My grandmother raised me."

"That must have been weird."

"Sometimes. Mostly, though, she's just like any parent. She might as well be my official guardian, not my mom. I don't know why she never formalized it. Maybe she didn't want to drag my mom into court."

"And your grandma also manages your career."

"Yeah," Shana said. "And lately she's been managing it to death."

"Why?"

"She says she wants to teach me new acting skills. She says I'll need them when I'm offered adult roles."

"That sounds logical."

"It is, except that I'm not even sure I want to *be* an adult actress!"

He studied her intently. "Whether or not you continue acting is your decision. But, remember, it's important to be yourself. No matter what, you've got to be true to who you are."

Shana nodded her head vigorously. That's exactly how I feel, she thought. My future is *my* choice, not my grandmother's. Why can she only see what she wants for me, and not what I want for myself? Won't she ever understand?

Kirk understood. He was the first boy she had ever met who could see what was in her heart. Suddenly she felt a rush of emotion that was more powerful than anything she had ever experienced before. Getting up, she went to the head of the bed and snuggled next to him. He put his arms around her, and she sighed.

"I love you," she said. For two days the words had been echoing in her mind, and now they came out easily.

Instantly he gathered her up in a powerful embrace. "Shana, you don't know how much I want to kiss you right now!" he gasped.

"Oh?" She pulled her head back a little. "Why don't you?"

"I don't want to give you my cold."

Suddenly she sat bolt upright. "Oh, my—Kirk, what time is it?"

He glanced at his watch. "Just about ten, why?"

"I was supposed to be home for a rehearsal at eight. My grandma is going to kill me!"

Springing up, she grabbed her purse and headed for the door.

"Hey, am I going to see you before Saturday?" Kirk called out.

"I don't know. I'll phone you tomorrow," she called back over her shoulder.

Two minutes later she was in the back of a taxi, heading home. Hanging on to an overhead strap, she sat on the edge of her seat the whole way. What would Edith say? What would she do? Was it possible that she herself had forgotten about the rehearsal? Shana could only hope.

At Sutton Place she paid the driver and dashed up the steps. Pushing open the heavy mahogany front door, she went inside. She had no chance to prepare herself. Edith was pacing up and down the marble-floored front hall.

Her grandmother's look could have frozen the entire East River. "You are late."

"Uh, sorry."

"Would you mind telling me where you've been? I've been sick with worry." There was a note of strain in her voice.

Shana decided that the best thing was to tell the truth. She hadn't wanted to tell her grandmother about Kirk just yet, but she didn't want her to think she had been getting into trouble either.

"I was with Kirk Tucker."

A silence descended in the hall. "You mean the tennis player who was in the studio last week?"

"Yes."

"Would you tell me *where* you went with him? To dinner? To a movie?" She studied her granddaughter. "To his hotel room?"

Shana tried to stay calm, but heat rushed to her face, giving her away. Edith collapsed in a red velvet chair and rubbed her forehead. It was several minutes before she spoke.

"Shana . . ." Her voice was softer than Shana had expected it to be. "Contrary to what you may think, I'm not angry about your adventure in Mr. Tucker's hotel room. After all, I know you understand the facts of reproduction—"

"Grandma, we weren't doing anything like that!" Shana cried, upset and embarrassed.

"What angers me," Edith went on, ignoring her outburst, "is that you didn't have the courtesy to phone. Anything might have happened to you!" She looked upset.

Shana was upset too. Why should Edith choose that moment to expect her to account for her whereabouts? Why should she have to be at Edith's beck and call? She crossed her arms defiantly, refusing to apologize. So what if she had lost track of time?

Rising, her grandmother drew herself up to her full height, which was considerable. At times like that, Shana felt like a dwarf by comparison. Edith crossed to the hall table and pressed a button. A bell sounded in the depths of the house.

Nora, their stout cook and housekeeper, appeared. "Yes, Miss Bradbury?"

"Nora, bring a pot of coffee and two cups into the front parlor, please. Shana and I are going to begin our rehearsal."

Shana glanced at the hall clock in horror. "We can't start *now*! It's ten-thirty!"

"We shall start whenever I say," her grandmother said icily. "Bring the coffee, Nora. Shana, follow me."

A moment later they began. Shana was seething. She couldn't believe it. Starting to work at that hour of the night was ridiculous.

Edith didn't seem to care about that. Opening her script to their first scene for the following day, she launched into the work. In an instant she was transformed into meek, helpless Betty Balfour.

A short while later there was a tap on the door. Nora pushed it open. "Your coffee," she said, setting a silver tray on a low table.

At 1:30 A.M. they were still at work. Shana was dead on her feet. The room was swimming around her, and her eyes could barely focus on her script.

"Grandma, can't we quit now?" she groaned.

Edith paused, looking up from her script. Her eyes were bright. "Certainly not. We have one more scene to run through."

"But I'm *tired*," Shana complained. "What good will it do if I fall asleep in the studio tomorrow?" Her shoulders slumped.

"You won't fall asleep. In fact, I think you'll perform rather well. Either way, we shall continue. You stay up partying far later than this most nights," Edith said in her steeliest voice. "Work comes before everything—boys and sleep included!"

Shana knew she was absolutely, positively going to die.

Ten

The next morning at seven-fifteen Shana arrived at work. Her grandmother had risen and left the house long before her. How does she do it? Shana wondered. Is the woman a robot, or what? She certainly isn't human!

Just as she was about to pull open the front door of the studio, she heard a gravelly voice call her name. She turned. "Yes?"

"Olivia Waxman from *TV Talk* magazine." A rumpled-looking woman was holding up a press identification card. "May I ask you a few questions?"

"I—" Shana hesitated. She was not supposed to give interviews that hadn't been approved by the publicity department, she knew. She also knew that *TV Talk* was not one of the better publications covering daytime TV. It was cheap, and its stories were of the scandal-seeking variety.

"It won't take a minute," Olivia Waxman pressed. "We're doing a feature on Mitch Callahan, and we need some background information."

At the mention of Mitch's name, Shana started. Before she was aware of it, she was saying, "Well, if it won't take too long . . ."

"Ten seconds, I promise."

It took a lot longer than that, naturally. The woman's questions were routine—at first. Shana answered them impatiently. She knew the woman could have learned most of what she was asking from network publicity releases.

Then Olivia Waxman flipped her steno pad closed. "Just off the record, Miss Bradbury, how does the cast feel about Mitch?" she asked.

"Okay, I guess. Everyone thinks he's perfect as Matt Davidson."

"Don't people find him hard to work with because of his temper?"

Shana frowned. How had the reporter known that? "The pressure gets to us all sometimes," she said tactfully.

"Do you know of any stories or rumors about him going around the studio?"

"Only the one about him being arrested for—" She tried to stop herself, but the damaging words were already out of her mouth.

"Arrested for what?" the reporter asked eagerly.

"For burglary, but that's only a rumor," Shana said emphatically.

The woman flipped open her steno pad and began to scribble furiously.

"Hey, why are you writing *that* down?" Shana objected. "What I just said was strictly off the record."

"It's not off the record unless you say so in advance," Olivia Waxman said, chuckling. "Thank you, Miss Bradbury. That was just the sort of lead I was hoping for!"

Half a second later Olivia Waxman hurried away. Shana was furious about being tricked—and nervous too. Would *TV Talk* print the rumor? It was possible. To a sleazy rag like that, even vague and ridiculous tidbits were big news.

But, no, she decided. She was worrying about nothing. The network would kill the story when the magazine called for confirmation. And even if it got printed, who cared? It wasn't true. All it would do would make Mitch squirm. And *that* was perfectly all right with her!

After she pulled open the studio door, she headed straight for her dressing room. Gradually her thoughts returned to her grandmother. She was still angry—not to mention exhausted—about their late-night rehearsal. This time Edith had gone too far. But what could she do? As long as the script kept them together, Edith was going to demand that they rehearse at home.

Suddenly, just as she was about to go through her door, Shana spotted a rotund figure waddling in her direction. It was Peter Ferris, the soap's head writer.

"Peter, how *are* you!" she cooed, skipping up to him.

She truly disliked the man. He was fat, prissy, and vain. She usually avoided him—but aside from Sally, he was the only person who could make changes in the soap's master story line.

"Well, Shana Bradbury! How are *you*?" He pinched her cheek between two stubby fingers.

She hid her revulsion. "Peter, I just *looove* the way you're developing my grandmother's idea. The story is totally fantastic!"

He beamed. "Thank you." Praise like that was his lifeblood.

"I mean, it's so touching the way Jasmin's helping Betty."

"You're doing a lovely job with it, too, dear," he said.

"Thank *you*. I was thinking, though, Peter, wouldn't it be better if Betty faced her problems alone?"

"Hmm—that's an interesting suggestion," he said, tapping a finger where his chin should have been. "Let me think, it *would* make her much more vulnerable. . . ."

Shana's heart beat faster. Was he really going to accept her idea and separate Betty and Jasmin?

If he did, her problems would be over. Anxiously, she held her breath.

"No, no—I'm sorry. Every character needs to have a friend, Shana. Otherwise they won't seem likable. Jasmin and Betty have to stay together."

Shana was crushed. Then a new thought struck her. "Peter, suppose Jasmin's psychic powers begin to fail—"

"So that she can't help Betty anymore?" Peter said, picking up her idea immediately. "Hey, I like that one!"

"It would put Betty in greater danger, you see?"

"Sure, and instead of using her sixth sense to protect Betty, Jasmin would have to rely on plain old logic."

"No, no! Jasmin would be out of the picture!" Shana objected, horrified.

But Peter didn't hear. He was lost in a creative reverie. "Yes, I can see it. Jasmin and Betty trapped by the killer—a dark room. . . ."

Shana felt the color drain from her face. He was taking her suggestion the wrong way! Instead of moving Jasmin and Betty apart, he would bring them together in new scenes.

She had to think of something—fast! "Peter, how about if the would-be killer injures Jasmin?" She hated violence, but at least it would knock Jasmin out of the story line.

"Wonderful twist!" Peter's face lit up. "Up to

now, Jasmin's helped Betty. Now Betty can nurse Jasmin. Oh, think of the sickbed scene we could have! Have you ever thought of becoming a writer, dear?"

Groaning, Shana decided to give up. Every new suggestion was only producing more rehearsals for her and Edith, not fewer.

"Must go put this in my word processor," Peter muttered as he hurried away. "Thanks, Shana. If you ever stop acting, come and work for me as an episode writer!"

"I might do that," she called after him. Now she felt worse than ever!

Shana didn't think her day could get any worse, but it did.

That afternoon she stood to one side as Katie and Mitch rehearsed a scene. It was an important one to the story, because in it Matt Davidson again gave in to his obsession for Alicia Gately, the poor, sexy teen temptress who would do anything to get her way.

As she watched, Shana marveled at how Katie and Mitch handled that stock soap opera situation. Matt was not just a rich boy in love with the wrong girl: he was a young man torn between a desire to do right and a need to act on his feelings. Alicia was no simple vixen: she was a girl tragically searching for love and security in the only way she knew how.

Together, they sizzled.

Slowly Shana became aware that there was a special chemistry between them. Katie, especially, brought to the scene a depth of feeling that made it seem real.

Then it hit her. She understood why Katie was able to make her performance so convincing. Katie was really in love with Mitch!

And, she realized, Katie must have been in love with him since she had first appeared on the show, even while she, Shana, had been dating him!

After the final taping that day, Shana went straight to Katie's dressing room and sat waiting for her. She hadn't bothered to change and remove her makeup. She was too angry and hurt to think about that.

"Shana!" Katie smiled as she came in, but her face fell as soon as she noticed Shana's expression. "Hey, what's wrong? You look like you're mad at me."

"Mad doesn't even begin to describe it," Shana said, her voice shaking. "How could you have lied to me, Katie? How could you have done that?"

"I don't know what you're talking about," Katie said nervously, shutting her door. Sitting on her makeup stool, she looked at Shana with genuine puzzlement.

"You don't know? Okay, then, I'll spell it out," she said, her voice tight. "You're in love with Mitch, and you have been since day one. You let me go on and on about him—"

"Shana, don't be ridiculous." Katie laughed, but the sound was false.

"You deny it?"

"I'd like to know what makes you think I am?" she asked, dodging the question.

Shana crossed her arms. As she watched, Katie tossed her head, sending her silky blond hair floating over one shoulder.

"A lot of things make me think so," she began. "Mostly it's what I saw in rehearsal today. You couldn't have made that scene so convincing unless you were really in love with him."

"That's crazy!"

"Oh, yeah? I've been an actress a lot of years, lady, and believe me, I know what goes into a dynamite performance like that—your own feelings."

Katie said nothing.

"There were other things that tipped me off too," she went on.

"Such as?"

"Your tears over that teensy insult yesterday—your perfect boy fantasy—the way you hung up the phone after you said you wanted to see him suffer."

Katie's jaw tightened. Rising, she began to unbutton her costume. She was trying to stay cool, Shana guessed, but she wasn't doing a very good job of it. Her fingers were trembling.

Then, just as she was reaching for the hanger on the back of her door, Katie suddenly snapped.

She whirled around, her blond hair a blur. Her eyes blazed even as tears began to pool in them.

"You're wrong, Shana! I'm not his girlfriend and never will be."

"Then you admit you love him?"

"I—yes, I love him, but what does it matter? He doesn't love me back. He—he *hates* me!" Her lower lip trembled.

Shana already knew the truth, but even so Katie's confession took her breath away. When she could speak again, she unleashed her feelings in a flood of resentment.

"I thought you were one person I could trust, and you lied to me! How could I have poured my heart out to you? I guess you thought it was pretty funny, huh? Dumb little Shana tearing herself up over Mitch while you—while you—"

While you what? Shana stopped and wondered. Katie hadn't gotten any more from Mitch than she had. In fact, she had gotten a lot less. It just isn't fair! she thought. What had given one lousy boy so much power over them anyway? Blinded by her tears, she spun around and slapped the chair behind her. It fell over with a clatter. Then she was crying—hot, wracking sobs.

Katie was crying, too, her face in her hands. "Shana, I'm sorry—I never wanted to hurt you."

Shana's heart softened. Going to Katie, she put her arms around her friend. They cried together until the tears had run out.

Finally Shana glanced in the mirror. They were quite a sight: two girls, faces streaked with mascara, clinging to each other in desperation.

She pulled away with a little laugh. "Well, looks like we're both losers where Mitch is concerned," she said.

"Yeah, I guess so," Katie said miserably. She looked utterly devastated.

Shana felt a rush of sympathy for her. "I guess it's worse for you though. You're still in love with him."

"You're not exactly over him either," Katie pointed out.

"I never cared about him the way I do about Kirk. It's just that he hurt me so much."

Katie wiped under each eye with a tissue. "Shana," she asked. "Are you sure Mitch is in love?"

"Yes," she replied, righting the chair. "That's the one thing I still don't understand. If it's not you, then who is it?"

"I wish I knew!" Katie groaned.

One thing was for sure, Shana thought. They weren't going to find out from Mitch!

A short while later Shana hugged her friend goodbye and went to her own dressing room. She was glad that she and Katie had cleared the air. It had been horrible to live with suspicions about her best friend even for one day.

At the same time, things between them were not exactly the same as they had been, she realized. Previously, she had believed that Katie was completely incapable of deception. But it wasn't true. Katie could keep a secret—even deceive her.

Would she ever be able to trust anyone, one hundred percent, ever again?

Eleven

In the two days that followed Shana began to resent her at-home rehearsals with Edith more than ever. The reason was Kirk. She wanted to spend every free minute with him, but Edith's schedule made it impossible.

The real problems had begun the day after her fight with Katie. She and Kirk had met for lunch at a Chinese restaurant near the studio. They had a wonderful time; Kirk's cold was getting better and he swore it was because of Shana. He had even mentioned the possibility that he would rent an apartment in New York to use as a base during his upcoming tour. Then, after their fortune cookies had arrived at the end of the meal, he had dropped a bombshell.

"Shana, we need to talk. I think we should be careful about getting too involved," he told her.

"What?"

"You know what I mean," he said, looking down in embarrassment. "This past week has been fantastic, but it won't last. After the tournament ends on Saturday, I'll be back on the road."

Panic gripped her. "Kirk, we'll see each other again! You're coming back here in September for the U.S. Open. That's not so far away."

"But what about after that?" he pressed. "Having a traveling tennis pro for a boyfriend isn't going to be much fun for you."

"We'll work it out. What about the idea you had before about renting an apartment here?"

"That's not definite," he explained. "I have to talk to my coach about it, and he probably won't even like the idea."

She toyed with the edge of her napkin unhappily. "Kirk, you're scaring me! I can't lose you now—not when I've just found you."

"I'm not saying we have to lose each other. All I'm saying is that we should think about what we're getting into."

His words had not reassured her at all. Right then she had resolved to spend as much time as possible with him before Saturday, when he had to leave for his next tournament, the ATP Championship in Cincinnati. If she did that, she hoped, then maybe he'd get more comfortable with the idea of them as a couple. He'd see that what they had could last.

But spending time—real time—with Kirk was a virtual impossibility when Edith expected her to be home rehearsing every night. Shana hadn't seen him since their Chinese lunch. He had had to spend the next day in Forest Hills, playing the first round of the charity tournament. When he had returned after dinner, they talked on the phone for an hour. But that wasn't the same—she needed to *see* him.

Now, on Friday morning, Shana had a plan. She rose at 5:45 A.M., fifteen minutes earlier than usual. In her bed clothes—a pair of underpants and a T-shirt—she dropped to the floor and began doing rapid sit-ups.

Earlier that summer Katie had persuaded her to visit a health club once, but she hadn't gone back. Now she was glad. Out of shape, she was hot and perspiring in no time. After doing a hundred jumping jacks for good measure, she slipped back into bed and began to moan.

Edith gasped as she pulled the thermometer from Shana's mouth. "Oh, no! Your temperature's quite high, I'm afraid, dear."

Shana suppressed a smile. She knew that already. While her grandmother had gone out of the room to fix a cold cloth for her forehead, she had touched the tip of the thermometer to the light bulb in her bedside lamp. In seconds her temperature had shot up to one hundred and four degrees.

In a quavery voice, Shana said, "I'd better get dressed for work." She began to pull down her covers, but Edith stopped her.

"No. You're staying home today."

"But, Grandma, I can't! We've got scenes to tape, remember?"

Edith seemed deeply touched by her grand-daughter's display of professional pride. She smiled gently. "Shana, the scenes that aren't essential to the story will be cancelled. The others we can tape next week. I'll arrange it."

A shout of triumph nearly escaped her mouth, but she bit it off. It was perfect! Exactly what she had wanted. She writhed and groaned a little to cap her act.

"Oh, dear." Alarmed, Edith reached for Shana's phone. "I'm going to send for a nurse to stay with you," she announced.

"No!" Shana sat up, even more alarmed than her grandmother. "I mean, you don't have to. Nora will take care of me."

"It's Nora's day off," Edith reminded her. "She left last night to visit her relatives in New Jersey."

"Well, I'll be okay on my own, Grandma," Shana assured her.

"Nonsense, you're too sick to be left alone."

"Really! I mean it! Besides, I don't want some nurse fussing over me all day."

Edith wavered. "Hmm—perhaps I can phone you from the studio to see how you are.

That way, if you're feeling bad I can have a nurse come."

"No, please don't even call. I think I'd just like to stay in bed and sleep," Shana lied.

"Promise me you'll take aspirin and drink liquids?" Edith said.

"I promise."

Smiling, her grandmother sat down beside her and took her hand. In her bathrobe and slippers she almost looked like a real grandmother, Shana thought. A guilty pang shot through her as she realized how completely she was deceiving Edith, but she ignored it. She had to do it for the sake of her sanity.

"Shana, if this happened because we've been working too hard, I'm very sorry," Edith said. "You know how much I care about you."

Shana held in a surge of anger. "Yes, I know."

Is she kidding me? Shana thought. As soon as I'm "well," we'll be back to the same old routine. Still, she was touched by her grandmother's display of affection—more than she wanted to be.

An hour after Edith left for the studio, Shana was up, showered and dressed in her summer best: a pair of white stirrup pants, an oversize shirt cinched in with a big belt, and sneakers. Her hair was pulled back into a long ponytail, and a sporty white sun visor circled her head.

Sliding a pair of Laura Biagiotti sunglasses on her face, she slipped out the front door and headed for the street. She wasn't exactly sure how to get to Forest Hills—she was a Manhattan girl, after all. But she was sure a cab driver would know.

The ride to Forest Hills took no time at all, and the driver found the tennis stadium quickly. She had to ask how to get to the men's locker room several times. But soon she was in the lounge outside the men's locker room, waiting for a reply to the note she had sent back to Kirk.

In less than a minute Kirk appeared. "Shana!" he said, smiling broadly as she ran into his arms. "Is this getting to be a habit, or what?"

"What do you mean?" she asked into his shirt. It felt wonderful to wrap her arms around him.

"Showing up unexpectedly. First you barged into my dressing room, then my hotel room—now you're here too."

"Just wait till I get to know you better. You won't be safe anywhere."

He laughed. "Seriously, the ticket I gave you is for tomorrow. What are you doing here today?"

"I got the day off, so I thought I'd come out and wish you luck," she said simply.

"Can you stay?"

"Sure."

"Then hold on."

He went back inside the locker room. Five minutes later he was back. He handed her a front row ticket for his match.

"It's on the sunny side of the stadium, but I didn't think you'd mind," he said.

"Mind? Are you kidding?"

They talked for a few minutes more, until Kirk's coach, a robust man in his forties named Larry Hillyard, came out. Kirk introduced them, and then Larry informed him it was time to warm up.

"Good luck!" Throwing her arms around him again, Shana gave him an eye-opening kiss right in front of his coach. Kirk blushed furiously, but he looked pleased, too, she noticed.

Inside the stadium, Shana stopped short when she saw the TV cameras that would broadcast the game live over a New York channel. The last thing she wanted was to be seen on TV! What if her grandmother saw the program?

Then her fears melted away. If they did do a pan of the crowd, she'd just be one speck among thousands—totally unrecognizable. Besides, Edith would never see a live broadcast like this one. She was at work.

She was reading her program when Gloria Ziegler walked across the court and stopped in front of her.

"Hi, Shana, long time no see," she said and smiled. Gloria was a short, shapely woman with honey-colored hair.

"Hi, Gloria!" Then Shana jumped to the subject of greatest interest to her. "How do you like playing with Kirk?"

Gloria twirled her racquet. "It's great—except for one thing. All he wants to talk about is a certain soap star we both know."

"Really?" She was sure she would die from happiness right on the spot.

"Let's just say that you've got his attention in a big way," Gloria reported. "Congratulations. He's a nice guy."

"Thanks. And good luck too."

Gloria wiped her forehead with her terry wristband. "I hope I get through it. I feel about as peppy as an armadillo on a cold morning."

A short while later the match began. Shana didn't know the rules very well, but she was quickly caught up in the drama. Each point was like a little play, she discovered. There were beginnings, middles, and ends, as well as reversals, comic interludes, and brink-of-disaster rescues—all without a single word being spoken.

Her heart pounded especially hard whenever the ball landed in Kirk's side of the court. He rarely failed to return it though. At one point he even brought the crowd to its feet. It happened during a crucial point in the second set. Catching him out of position, the pro on the opposite team sent a high lob to the back corner of the court. The ball bounced, then soared deep over the out-of-court apron. The crowd applauded, thinking the point was over, but then Kirk streaked toward it, nearly running into the seats. With a quick, stunning backward flip of his racquet, he sent the ball sailing back over the net, saving the point.

The crowd cheered, Shana hardest of all. She leapt to her feet, applauding, flushed with pride and admiration.

Kirk and Gloria won their match, and afterward they all had lunch together in the stadium's VIP lounge. Shana stayed for the semifinal match that afternoon too. The pair won that one as well, but not without some difficulty. Midway through the final set, Gloria sat on a bench and tucked her head between her knees, obviously feeling unwell.

It was during this time out that Shana got a shock. Lifting her eyes from her program, she saw that a remote TV crew had focused their Minicam on her. Filling the time with crowd shots, they had picked her out for a close-up. She was on the air.

With an anxious jolt, she quickly stuck her sunglasses on her face. How did *that* happen? she wondered. It didn't matter, of course, but even so it made her nervous. She was glad when Gloria, shaken but okay, returned to the game.

Later, Shana congratulated Kirk in the men's locker room lounge. He was hot and sweaty, but that didn't matter to her in the least.

"Coming again tomorrow?" he asked, wiping his face with a towel.

"Wouldn't miss it," she confirmed. Then she glanced at the clock on the wall. It was four-thirty: time for her to head home.

As she prepared to go, however, Kirk looked puzzled. "What's the hurry?"

"I've got to be there when my grandma gets home," she told him.

"Rehearsal?"

"Well, no—"

"Shana what's bothering you?" He sensed right away that something was wrong.

Quickly Shana explained the trick she had pulled and then told him about the remote Minicam. "I know it's impossible for my grandma to have seen the broadcast. But what if someone else saw it and tells her?"

"Shana, I don't believe you did that!"

"But I just wanted to be with you," she said, a lump in her throat.

"You shouldn't have run out on your responsibilities like that, even if it was to see me."

"Well, thanks a lot," she growled. "I went to all that trouble, and now you're giving me a lecture. I don't need it."

"Yeah? Well, I don't need to be the cause of trouble between you and your grandmother, Shana. She's going to think I'm bad news."

"Come on, she'll never find out about it."

"You'd better hope not!"

They kept up their heated exchange until Shana couldn't bear to stay a second longer. She kissed Kirk and got a salty and very unsatisfying kiss. She ran out and looked for a cab. They were all taken, so she walked to the subway station, feeling horrible.

Everything's crazy, she thought. I came to Forest Hills to help cement our relationship, and now, thanks to me, it may be almost over. Thank goodness I'll be able to talk to Kirk again tomorrow, she comforted herself. Maybe by then he won't still be angry.

As Shana rushed to drop a token into the subway turnstile, a train pulled out of the station, leaving her behind. It was not a good omen, she decided.

Shana's throat was tight as she pushed open her front door. It was almost six o'clock. Had Edith come home yet?

The house was utterly silent as she entered. She relaxed. She had worried about nothing, she could see now. Final taping was rarely finished that early, and even if it was it would be unusual for her grandmother to rush home from the studio. She decided to fix a snack.

Twenty minutes later she was in the breakfast room, eating milk and cookies. Suddenly the door flew open. Edith rushed in. Without a word, she felt her granddaughter's forehead.

"Hey, Grandma, isn't it great?" Shana said, bubbling. "I feel all better."

Edith's mouth was a tight line. "Going to Forest Hills speeded your recovery, no doubt."

Shana choked on some milk. When she had recovered she turned hesitantly toward her grandmother. Her voice was a nervous squeak. "H-how did you find out? You never watch tennis!"

"No, but your friend Katie Nolan does. She turned on the TV in the studio lounge."

Shana made a mental note to murder her friend, then tried to cover herself. "Grandma, it was the funniest thing," she lied. "Just half an hour after you left this morning my fever went away. There was no point going to work, I figured, since the scenes were being cancelled, so I—"

Edith brought her fist down on the table, making the cookies jump. "Don't play games with me, Shana. I'm not in the mood."

"Grandma, I—"

"You're lying, and you know it!" Edith shouted. "That sickbed scene this morning was a sham."

Shana sat silently, looking down at her hands. There were times to speak and times to shut up, she knew—and that was definitely a time to shut up.

The performance that followed had to rank as one of the greatest of Edith's career, Shana decided later. It was awesome how incredibly small her grandmother made her feel. After discussing responsibility, commitments, and the family tradition, she moved on to her own, personal humiliation. Then she explained how carefully she had covered for Shana so she wouldn't be fired.

Shana felt like a total worm.

Finally Edith's tirade ended. Her chest heaving, her eyes fiery with rage, she asked, "Do you have anything to say for yourself?"

She didn't. Anything she said would only make her grandmother angrier.

"Very well, then. Starting right now, and until further notice, you are grounded!"

★

Twelve

It wasn't being grounded that bothered Shana. She supposed she had earned it. What did bother her was being grounded *now*. With Kirk due to leave New York the following afternoon, Edith's punishment definitely fell into the cruel and unusual category.

Naturally she had tried to explain that to her grandmother, and naturally Edith had not understood. Even when she had pleaded to be allowed to see Kirk off at the airport—something she had been counting on—Edith had been adamant.

"Allow you to visit the boy who started this in the first place? You must be joking, Shana," she had scoffed.

"Grandma! It's *important* to me!"

"And honoring your studio contract isn't? Young lady, it seems to me that your priorities are in an even bigger mess than your room. Why don't you go upstairs and try to straighten out both? It will do you good."

Shana had stormed up to her room and slammed the door as hard as she could.

Now it was two hours later. Her room was still a mess, but her priorities were becoming clearer by the minute—she had to see Kirk again before he left New York. If she didn't, she might as well kiss their relationship goodbye—especially after their fight that afternoon.

But how could she? There was no hope of sneaking away from the house on a weekend, she knew. Edith would be guarding the front door. Neither was there any hope of changing Edith's mind—not after that scene downstairs. The situation was hopeless.

Sinking into a chair, Shana wracked her brains. Long, rectangular patches of sunlight crept across her carpet as the sun sank toward the horizon. She turned her stereo on full blast, then turned it off. Nothing seemed to help. She couldn't come up with a plan.

Finally she gave up and phoned for Chinese food. On Nora's days off, she and Edith fended for themselves, either eating in restaurants or sending for take-out food. When her sesame noodles arrived she paid the delivery boy and started up the two flights of stairs to her room, feeling depressed.

Then midway between the first and second floors, she stopped in her tracks. On the wall next to her were portraits of all the great Bradburys, from her great-great-grandfather Horace Bradbury—who had once shared a bill with John Wilkes Booth—to her mother, Barbara. Suddenly she had an idea.

Dashing to her room, she frantically searched the top of her desk. Somewhere in the tide of letters, scripts, and magazines was her mother's most recent phone number. It was a Paris number, she remembered. Barbara was in France trying to raise money for yet another comeback film.

When she found the scrap of paper, she jumped on her bed, scooped up her phone, and started punching buttons.

Just before she pushed the final number, she paused. Is this really such a good idea? she wondered. Her plan was to ask Barbara to intercede with Edith—even overrule her, if necessary. As her official guardian, her mother had the power to do that. But would Barbara understand? Would she even care about her daughter's problem?

The fact was, she barely knew her mother. She saw her maybe once a year, and when she did it was like meeting a stranger—a beautiful, intense stranger. Except for her father, whom

Shana had never met, and whom her mother had divorced, they had little in common.

Finally, though, she pushed the final button. I'm desperate, she decided. The phone on the other side of the ocean began to ring. As it did, Edith walked into her room.

"Don't bother," Edith said simply. "She isn't there."

"How do you know who I'm calling?" Shana demanded. The fear she had felt during Edith's earlier tirade had faded a little.

Edith gestured toward the strange-looking phone number on Shana's lap. "Who else would you be calling overseas?" she reasoned.

The phone continued to ring. Turning away from her grandmother, Shana thought, Come on—pick it up, Mom! Pick it up!

For two full minutes the ringing went on. Shana hung up, disappointed. "How did you know she wouldn't be there?" she asked Edith.

"Because of this." She tossed the copy of the New York *Post* she was carrying on the bed. On the front page was a blurry black-and-white photo of a disheveled-looking woman being hauled into a police van. The policemen were French, and the woman in the picture was her mother.

"Oh, no!" A gasp of horror and dismay escaped her. With trembling fingers she opened the paper and read the story inside. The facts were gruesome, but clear: drunk and disorderly

. . . recent collapse of a film deal . . . long history of public scenes. . . .

Fear, disbelief, shock, and humiliation all mixed together in Shana, leaving her speechless. She was angry too. Once again her mother wasn't there for her.

When she looked up again, Edith had left the room. Thank goodness, Shana thought, rising to shut the door. She didn't want her grandmother to see her cry. . . .

Later Shana punched in the number of Kirk's hotel on her phone. She didn't want to call him; she wanted to *see* him. But she couldn't, she had accepted that by then. At least by phoning him, she told herself, I can explain why I won't be at the match tomorrow—or at the airport after that.

"I'm sorry, there's no answer in that room."

Shana slammed the receiver back in its cradle. Where is he? she wondered miserably. Not only can't I see him, I can't talk to him either!

Rising, she went to her window. The sun was down, and slowly the city was turning into a world of black voids and bright, cheerless lights. Alone and cut off from the boy she loved, she was sure that that was the lowest moment of her life.

By eleven o'clock on Saturday morning, Shana had still not reached Kirk. She had lain down the night before to rest for a minute but fell asleep until eight o'clock in the morning.

She had phoned his hotel when she woke up, but the front desk had informed her that he had already checked out. Then she left half a dozen messages at the tennis stadium. He hadn't returned her calls. She assumed it was because he was busy, but if he wasn't—well, she didn't want to think about that.

Now there was just an hour to go before his final match was scheduled to begin. Why doesn't he *call*! she wondered in panic. He was due to go to the airport right after his match, which wouldn't leave any time to phone. He had to phone *before* he played. If he didn't, she wouldn't get to talk to him at all!

Slowly the minutes ticked by. Shana began to play a game with herself. Before the clock's minute hand reaches three he'll phone, she told herself. When he didn't, she convinced herself he would phone by the time it hit five. But that didn't work either! Where *was* he?

Finally there was nothing to do but turn on her television to watch the match. He wasn't going to phone; that much was obvious. Maybe he was assuming she'd be in the stands; maybe he didn't care. She didn't know what to believe.

As the picture filled in, Shana recognized the green grass and white boundary lines of the Forest Hills exhibition court. She recognized Kirk, too, warming up. Her heart gave a powerful tug. And there was Gloria, smiling gamely for the camera.

Kirk and Gloria played their hardest, but even Shana could tell that Gloria was unwell. She kept pausing before each serve to press the back of her hand to her forehead. It was no surprise to Shana when they lost the match.

Her surprise came afterward when Kirk was interviewed. He defended Gloria's performance and said good-naturedly that his own playing was at fault, which Shana didn't believe for a moment. He had been superb.

Then the interviewer asked about his love life. "So whose heart have you been breaking lately, Kirk? Is she here today?"

Kirk just smiled. "Nope."

"But he was expecting her," Gloria put in anxiously, as though to assure the audience that Kirk did have a girlfriend. Kirk just gave her a somewhat pained grin and then changed the subject. A moment later the sportscaster moved on to the winning team.

Shana sat up and snapped off the set. Kirk thought she had stood him up! That did it! Edith's bossiness had gone far enough. It was ruining her only chance at happiness. She had to get away from her grandmother's iron rule.

But I can't get away from Edith, Shana thought. She *is* my guardian, in everything but name. I can hardly go running to my mother.

But there was one thing she could do: quit "Glitters." Edith barely cared what Shana did outside of acting, didn't she?

Shana rushed to her door and ran down the stairs. Her grandmother was in the front parlor, or Basic Training Grounds, as Shana had come to think of it. Unaware of her granddaughter's crisis, she was reading a book and sipping a cup of tea.

"Grandma, I have something to tell you," Shana blurted out as she burst through the door. She felt her jaw working.

Edith didn't appear surprised to see her. On the contrary, her casually raised eyebrow suggested that she had been expecting her granddaughter's outburst. "Oh?"

"I'm quitting 'Glitters.' I've had enough!"

"That is a rash statement, and I'm sure you don't mean it," Edith said, stirring her tea.

"Oh, yes, I do! I'm sick of rehearsing day and night. I'm sick of not having time to myself. And I'm sick of having to work with *you*! From now on, *I* am going to come first, not some lousy soap opera. My life is going to revolve around *me*, not the stuff you tell me to do."

Edith nodded. "I see. And when you leave the show, what will you do?"

"What normal kids do," Shana declared, planting her hands on her hips. "Eat, sleep, go to school, have fun—"

"Go out with boys?"

"Yes, that too! Especially that. Do you get the picture?"

Looking down, Edith turned a page in her book. "Yes, dear. It sounds very nice."

Shana couldn't stand Edith's cool indifference. Marching up, she snatched the book from her grandmother's hands. "Grandma, I'm *serious*. I'm quitting the show!"

"Really?" Edith's irritation barely showed. "When?"

"Right now. You can tell them on Monday that I'm not coming back. Ever."

Edith rose. "I'll do no such thing. Even if I were to permit such a thing, which I won't, you would still have to give adequate notice."

"Permit? *Permit!* You don't own me. You can't dictate my life."

"No, but I know this little temper tantrum won't last either."

Shana narrowed her eyes. "Oh, no? Well, let me tell you something, I'm going to quit acting. For good." She felt a pang as she said the words.

"Don't be ridiculous."

"What's ridiculous about it?" Shana shouted, close to tears. "Where will acting ever get me? If I fail at it, I'll be like—like my mother. If I succeed, I'll be like you, a lonely old legend with a scrapbook for a soul."

Her whole body was trembling. Her words had been hurtful, she knew, but she wasn't going to take them back. They were true enough.

Edith pressed her lips together until they were a thin, colorless line. Crossing her arms, she stared into Shana's eyes.

"Before you say anything more, I think you should cool off and do some serious thinking," she advised.

"I already have! I'm quitting acting."

"I doubt that. Remember, you are a Bradbury. Acting is in your blood. You won't throw away your heritage just like that."

"Oh, no?" Shana screamed. "Just watch me!"

With that, she threw her grandmother's book onto the chair and ran from the room.

Upstairs, she pulled an oversized leather tote bag from her closet and began to fill it with clothes. She added shoes, makeup, her steam iron, hair curlers, and jewelry.

Then lugging the bag, she trudged down the stairs and out the front door, past an open-mouthed Edith. I'll show her what's in my blood, she declared to herself. Freedom!

★

Thirteen

Kennedy Airport was busy that afternoon. Shana, however, was not. After finding a cash machine for her bank and augmenting her money supply, she had a lot of time to kill. She had arrived at three o'clock, but Kirk's flight was not until five. Sitting in a plastic seat, she waited—and thought.

What will Cincinnati be like? she wondered. There were tennis courts there, obviously. But it didn't really matter what it would be like. As long as she was with Kirk, she would be happy. Wouldn't she?

Restless, she scanned a newspaper and watched the hands of the clock overhead go around. Where was he, anyway? At four-thirty she began to get worried. He didn't seem like the kind of guy who would arrive late for a flight. Could something have happened to him? No. She wouldn't let herself think about that.

At four forty-five the flight began to board. She had already bought her ticket to save time.

Finally at six minutes to five, she spotted him hurrying toward the check-in counter, a bag in each hand. Her heart leapt. It's really happening, she thought. We really are going to fly away together!

Then she noticed Larry Hillyard behind him, and she wasn't quite so enthusiastic. She had forgotten about his coach.

"Kirk?"

He whirled around, startled, "Shana? I don't believe it. What are you doing here? Why weren't you at—" He stopped as he noticed the tote bag at her feet. "Hey, what's going on?"

"I'm coming with you," she said, forcing a smile she had not expected to force. She waited for his answering grin.

It never came. "You mean you're coming to Cincinnati?"

"Of course to Cincinnati. Where did you think?"

"Oh. Look, Shana—"

Just then Larry came up, glancing at his watch. He smiled as he saw her, then frowned as he saw her tote bag. He shot Kirk a questioning glance.

"Larry, I need a minute here. There's something I've got to straighten out."

Larry shrugged. "Okay, but let's hustle. That baby flies in five minutes."

Holding Shana's elbow, Kirk led her to one side. There was a curious mixture of admiration and sadness in his blue eyes.

He cleared his throat. "Shana, you can't come with me."

She felt as if her last hope had crumbled. "What do you mean? Why not?"

"It wouldn't work for me. Not right now, at any rate."

"I knew it!" she cried. "It's that fight we had yesterday, isn't it? You don't care about me anymore. You want to dump me. I bet you even told the operator at your hotel not to put through my call."

"What are you talking about?"

Shana looked down. "I phoned you last night."

"Shana," Kirk said, smiling and shaking his head. "I was with my *manager*. He dragged me out to do a publicity appearance."

Kirk came closer. "Now where did you get the goofy idea that I don't care about you—of course I care about you."

"Then why can't I go with you to Cincinnati?"

"Because—"

"If money's the problem, don't worry. I've got five hundred in cash and a ton of money in the bank and credit cards. I can pay my own way, see?" Shana said, holding up her ticket.

"It's not money, Shana, or anything like that. It's you and me. We're not ready for something like this."

"Sure we are. We're in love, aren't we?"

"Yeah, but what you're talking about is a whole lot more than love. It's a big commitment, you know what I mean?"

She took a deep breath. "I'm ready."

"I wasn't talking about that," he said, turning red.

"Then what were you talking about?"

"Our careers, for one thing. How can you travel with me and still work on 'All That Glitters'?"

"I can't—I already thought about that. That's why I quit."

"You *what*?"

"It's true," she confirmed. "And this morning I told my grandmother something else too—I said I was getting out of acting for good."

Kirk's face grew hard. "Now I *know* you can't go with me. Shana, listen—"

"Kirk! You don't mean that!"

They were interrupted by Kirk's coach. Larry was standing at the gate, pointing frantically at his watch.

"Shana, I've got to go or I'm going to miss my flight. Just trust me. If you came with me today— well, it just wouldn't be right."

"Kirk, *please!*" she pleaded, not caring that she was acting like a fool.

"I'm sorry, Shana." Kirk gave her a quick kiss goodbye. "I've really got to go!"

With that, he scooped up his bags and disappeared through the gate.

Her every instinct was to run after him. But her legs wouldn't obey her command to move. They were rooted to the spot.

A minute later his plane pulled away from the terminal. Standing at a large window, she watched it taxi to the end of a runway, wait in line, then finally go rushing forward. As it lifted into the air, her heart seemed to sink right through her body.

She went back to the molded plastic seat she had been in all afternoon, sat down, and stared at her sneakers. All my life, she thought, all I ever wanted was for someone to love me. But nobody ever has. Not really. Not when it counted.

One by one she thought about all the people in her life. Kirk—Mitch—Edith—Barbara—her father—even Katie. One by one, she realized, all of them had either ignored her or betrayed her in some way. None of them loved her.

In fact, nobody loved her at all. She was totally alone. She was too hurt even to cry.

Fourteen

The following Saturday, at noon, Shana lay in bed wondering what to do with her day. Go shopping? Read? Watch television? Now that she was no longer grounded, there ought to be *something* worthwhile, she thought.

The truth was, nothing seemed very interesting. In fact, since she had quit "All That Glitters" all the fun stuff she had always wanted to do had slowly lost its appeal. Why go roller-skating when she could do that every day? Why shop when she already owned a closet full of clothes? She was already longing for school to start again.

Why even get up at all? she wondered listlessly. It was just another summer day. There would be plenty of others. She had just rolled over to go back to sleep when her phone rang.

Instantly she lunged to answer it. Maybe it's Kirk! she thought excitedly. She believed their relationship was over, but even so she couldn't help hoping each time the phone rang.

But it wasn't Kirk. It was Katie calling to commiserate about Kirk. But when Katie began talking about something that had happened the day before at the studio, Shana cut her off rather abruptly. "Katie, that's a scream! But listen, I have to run. I'll call you!" Then she hung up.

A minute later she rose and got dressed. Katie's call had made her realize she was hungry. And bored. Maybe a little breakfast will spark things up, she thought. She wandered slowly down the stairs.

"Morning, Grandma."

Edith was in the breakfast room reading a script. The moment Shana entered, she rose and silently walked from the room.

Shana felt her face grow hot with humiliation. It had been like that since the previous Sunday when, after four hours of arguing, she had finally convinced Edith that she was giving up acting. Her grandmother had hand-delivered Shana's letter of resignation to Sally Conners on Monday morning, and had barely spoken a word to her granddaughter since.

Her jaw tight, Shana buttered a croissant and smothered it in jam. So what? It's her loss, she thought. Still, she couldn't help being hurt. She was used to talking to her grandmother. Now she could remember dozens of happy conversations they had had around that table, sharing stories from work, laughing, and joking. She missed those days, though she would rather have died than admit it.

If only Kirk would phone! she thought in anguish. Thirty seconds of hearing his voice would make up for all of Edith's neglect. But he hadn't called. He wasn't going to either. She knew that. She was no fool. The scene at the airport had ended their relationship for good.

All at once, she had had enough. Dropping her croissant on her plate, she stood up and marched from the room. This is ridiculous! she thought as she stomped up the stairs to her room. Why get all bent out of shape over things that don't matter and people who don't care? There's more to life than Kirk, Edith, and "Glitters"! There's a whole world out there full of people, places, and experiences that could make me even happier than I've been before. All I have to do is find it!

But where to begin? Looking around her room, she searched for an idea. Then her eyes came to rest on the tennis racquet she had bought for her match with Kirk. Of course! she thought. Why not really teach myself to play? She wasn't very athletic, true, but that could change. Millions of people enjoyed the game—why couldn't she enjoy it too?

Ten minutes later she was galloping down the stairs in shorts and sneakers, a can of balls in one hand and a towel and her wallet in the other. As she turned down the final flight, she ran straight into Edith.

She froze.

Her grandmother stared at her, a faintly puzzled look on her face. It was the most expression Shana had seen on her face in days.

"Grandma, I'm going to the tennis courts in Central Park. I'll be back later, okay?" In spite of herself, her heart began to pound.

"Fine." Her grandmother continued up the stairs, heading for her room.

That did it. Shana swore to herself that she would never care what Edith thought again. If her grandmother wasn't going to make any effort to reconcile their differences, then why should she?

Bouncing the last of her three balls, Shana stiffly swung her racquet. *Thunk*. The ball arced over the net, bounced, and rolled into the chain link fence. There. Now you're getting the hang of it, she told herself. All three went over that time.

Walking to the other side of the court, she collected the balls and hit them back in the other direction. *Thunk. Thunk. Thunk.* It was boring playing without a partner, she had long since concluded. She should have called Katie back and invited her to play, but she didn't want to hear about the show.

Shaking her head, Shana crossed the court to collect the balls. She was *not* going to think about "Glitters," she reminded herself.

Overhead, the sun was bright and hot. It was a lovely summer day—lazy and quiet, even for New York. Perfect ice cream weather. I'll go get some when my hour is up, she decided. There was a Häagen-Dazs store down on Columbus Avenue, not far from the place where she and . . .

Stop it!

Why am I constantly thinking about Kirk? she wondered. What's so great about Kirk, anyway? Who needs a guy like that?

She did, that was who. In a rush of anger and sorrow she realized that she missed Kirk terribly. Why did I ruin it all? Shana wondered. But why didn't he care enough to call me?

Suddenly furious, she bounced a ball and swung her racquet with all her might.

"Nice shot."

She turned around and looked in the direction of the voice, frowning. It didn't seem possible, but there he was! Kirk! Racquet in hand and in his tennis clothes, standing just inside the fence, he looked more wonderful than ever.

But joy and anger mixed and made it impossible for her to speak. After all, she had seen Kirk's expression. Why, he's enjoying this! she thought.

"Tucker!" she said angrily. "What the heck are you doing? Get off my court!"

"Not until we talk," Kirk said in an even voice.

Shana realized that Edith must have told Kirk where she could be found, and he grabbed a racquet and ran to find her. "It's too late, I don't want to talk now," she said, hearing her voice tremble. "Why couldn't you make one lousy phone call?"

"Shana. Please—"

"Just go away!"

She expected Kirk to answer, but instead, holding a tin pail filled with balls, he walked around her to the other side of the net. "You need a tennis partner," he said, reaching for a ball and then swinging his racquet. *Whooock!* The ball shot past Shana, bouncing once before clanging into the fence.

Shana narrowed her eyes. So he wanted to play games? She retrieved the ball and hit it toward Kirk with all her might.

Kirk returned the shot, running without strain. Again and again his shots whizzed by her. She kept swinging and running, missing most of what he hit. But she connected with some of the balls. They smashed into the net or soared out of sight. In frustration, she slammed two or three balls right at him. He returned them all.

Finally Shana was drained. After all her efforts, Kirk was still standing across the net, cool yet concerned, angry but understanding. He wasn't going to go away.

Shana walked up to the net. Kirk did too. They were face to face at last.

"Why *didn't* you call?" Shana asked again, barely able to hold back her tears.

Kirk reached over the net and tipped her chin up to look at her. "I could tell you I was too busy, Shana, but that wouldn't be true and you wouldn't believe it anyway." He sighed. "Come on, a tennis court is no place to talk like this."

He put his arm around her as they walked off the court and into the fieldhouse. Shana felt dizzy, he was so close. After he turned in the pail of balls, they walked out into the park.

"I didn't call," Kirk went on, "because I was afraid I wouldn't be able to give enough to us—"

"Kirk—" Shana felt her heart brimming with love for him.

"No, listen, Shana. This is important. I knew I wouldn't be seeing you very much, and I didn't know if that would be fair to us—to you. But now I've made a decision."

What decision? Shana thought, beginning to shake with dread. Has Kirk come all the way to New York to tell me he never wants to see me again?

"Y-you've made a decision?" she said.

Kirk stopped walking and turned to face her. "I missed you so much in Cincinnati. If you feel the same way about me . . ."

"Feel the same way?" Shana almost squealed, hugging him. "Of course I do! I've been doing a lot of thinking, too, and I'm pretty sure I understand why you couldn't take me with you. It wasn't just our relationship that was bothering you or the rotten way I'd been treating my grandmother—"

"Right," Kirk put in. "I realized later how upset you were because you felt she was pushing you too hard."

Shana stepped back and laughed. "That's putting it mildly!"

"My dad's put me through the mill at times. I've put *myself* through it too."

Shana nodded and they started walking again.

"Anyway," Kirk went on, "I saw you trying to throw your career away, and I felt that was wrong."

"But why? Aren't you the one who said that we've got to be true to ourselves?"

"Yes! Exactly!"

"Well, I *am*!" Shana maintained. "For the first time in my life I'm doing exactly what *I* want to do, not what other people tell me to do. Especially my grandmother—"

They walked over a rustic wooden bridge that crossed a stream. Walking in the opposite direction was a group of children holding silvery balloons.

"But are you happy?" Kirk asked softly when they were alone again.

Happy? His question caught her off guard. The truth was, in the past week she hadn't been thinking in terms of happy or sad. Mostly she had been viewing her life in terms of win or lose—Shana or Edith.

So, *am* I happy? she asked herself. She didn't know. It was okay to have lots of time off, that much she could say. But she did miss acting. She missed the lights, the excitement, the sense of accomplishment when taping was done. She missed being part of a team—of knowing that the success of "Glitters" had something to do with her.

There was something else, too: in the last few days she had been watching the show at home, like a regular viewer. Her own performance was good, she had noticed. Not great, but good. It was noticeably better. In fact, thanks to her grandmother, there had been a measurable improvement each day. She had a long way to go before she caught up with Katie, she knew, but that was okay. She was proud of what she had done, and she did want to do more.

"No, I guess I'm not happy," she told Kirk in answer to his question.

"Then you're not doing what you want to do," he declared. "And we both know what that is, I think."

"Acting."

She frowned. He was right, of course. But what about all the negative stuff? What about Edith and her outrageous rehearsals? Could she really put up with them again?

"Look at it this way," Kirk added. "Can you picture me without tennis?"

"No way!" She giggled. It was as much a part of him as his blue eyes and his golden blond hair.

"Well, that's how I feel about your acting. Sure, it's a drag at times, it's going to get in the way of other things. But it's also a big part of you. You wouldn't be who you are without it."

She sighed. "You're right, I guess. No, I *know* you're right. But will 'Glitters' take me back?" Inside, she was sure they would.

"You have to find out. But they do need you, right?"

"I guess. They *do* need Jasmin—and that's *me*, not some other actress."

Just then they emerged from the woods at the edge of The Lake. Ahead was the wrought-iron bridge. Laughing with a sudden, intense joy, she grabbed his hand and pulled him to its center. Then she grinned wickedly.

"Do you remember what happened the last time we stood here?"

"I came down with a cold," Kirk groaned.

"No! I mean right before that. I'd like a repeat performance, please."

He didn't need to be asked twice. In an instant he had swept her up in his arms and was kissing her passionately. She felt a familiar swirling begin inside her. It was delicious— sweeter than ten thousand scoops of Häagen-Dazs. It felt so good to be with him again!

A while later she leaned against him and sighed. "You know, you take direction well. Have you ever thought of becoming an actor?"

"No. But if you're performing I'll be the audience. Always."

Then he was kissing her again, and in her mind she heard an audience cheering.

★

Fifteen

"Good luck, Shana," Katie whispered, giving Shana's hand a squeeze.

It was six days later in the "All That Glitters" studio. Final taping had just begun, and as usual the cast was milling around in the outer corridor, waiting for their scenes.

Shana gave her friend's hand a squeeze back. She felt nervous, but it was a nice kind of nervous, she knew. It was wonderful being back on "Glitters."

That day the Jasmin-Betty plot line would reach a crucial turning point. In the next scene to be taped several startling facts would come out. Betty would learn who the killer stalking her

was, and the lives of several prominent Fairhope
residents would be changed as a result. The key
to all this was Jasmin, and Shana had a long,
complex speech to perform.

Pacing back and forth, Shana reviewed the
scene in her mind. When she was satisfied that
she had it down perfectly, she leaned against a
wall and pushed out an audible breath. She felt
good. Almost as good, she thought, as the day in
Sally Conners's office when the producer had told
her that she had not accepted her resignation
letter. She had instead marked her down for a
leave of absence.

"I knew you'd come back once you cooled
down," the producer had said. "The only question was, how long would it take?"

Not very long, as it turned out. A week and a
half after quitting she had been back on the show,
making up for lost time.

Just then the red light over the studio door
went out. That meant the first scene had been
taped. Next came hers. Shana tensed as Stu, the
assistant director, came out and read a list of
characters' names. "Okay, everyone inside."

The setting for the scene was a conference
room in the Fairhope police station. It was stark
and institutional looking—the perfect place to
strip souls bare.

Edith, who had been in the previous scene,
was already on the set. Shana's heart gave a big
thump as she spotted her. Although they had
performed together in the last few days, off the

set her grandmother was still distant. When will she ever stop being angry? Shana wondered.

"Places, everyone."

The scene began.

As she eased into the rhythm of the action, Shana felt a change come over her. Usually she felt an empathy with her character—a sort of blending. But that day it was different. That day she *was* Jasmin. Every line sprang from her mouth as if she was saying it for the first time. Every word came straight from her own heart.

Partly it was the training her grandmother had put her through, she knew, and partly it was the scene. In the past weeks, Jasmin and Betty had grown close. Jasmin had become Betty's protector and confidant.

But it was more than that. For the first time in her career, Shana was holding nothing of herself back. She knew that twelve million Americans would watch this scene, but that didn't matter in the least. If she goofed up, so what? A little mistake on screen was nothing compared to the big mistakes she had made in her own life recently.

Finally her long speech arrived. Shana poured everything she had into it—all her anguish, all her hope, all the love she had for the people in her life, Edith included.

As the scene ended, she placed one hand on Betty's shoulder in a gesture of compassion and friendship. The scene hadn't been blocked that way, but somehow it felt like the right thing to do.

A minute later she looked down at her grandmother, who was sitting in a chair. Would Edith break the silence that had separated them for so long? Would she forgive?

Edith's eyes showed nothing. Crushed, Shana turned and began to move away. Then a soft command stopped her.

"Shana, please stay."

Shana whirled around. It wasn't that her grandmother had spoken that touched her the most—it was her tone. She didn't sound like a drill sergeant or a school principal. Edith sounded just like herself—Shana's grandmother. The person who probably loved her more than anyone else in the world.

Without a word, she ran into her grandmother's outstretched arms.

"So, you see, all those rehearsals had a purpose," Edith said. "I really was trying to help you, Shana."

They were in Edith's dressing room, talking. Her scenes for the day over, Edith was removing her makeup with cold cream.

"Grandma, I know that already. What I don't get is *why*?"

Edith wiped away the last of the makeup. Her face was totally without adornment. Shana rarely saw her grandmother that way.

"It's because of your mother, to tell the truth," Edith confessed, turning to her. "For years I've felt guilty because of her."

Shana was surprised. "You have? Why? You and Mom don't get along at all!"

"Yes, that's true. She has rejected me about as completely as a daughter can. But that doesn't stop me from caring. I feel responsible for her failure as an actress. I feel that I should have done more to help her."

"In what way?"

"Well, you know all the comebacks she's been trying to make since she divorced your father?" Edith asked.

"Uh-huh." Not one of them had been successful, Shana knew.

"The reason they've all bombed is that she hasn't got the discipline she needs. She thinks she can get by on the things that made her a sex symbol during the sixties—looks, family reputation, and a degree of raw talent."

Shana was beginning to understand. "So you feel that if you had only taught her the *craft* of acting, she wouldn't be having such a hard time right now."

"Yes."

"And that if you taught *me* those skills, then I'd never have the same problems as her."

"Right again. I've tried to give you *some* freedom—but where your career is concerned, I couldn't stand by and let you make mistakes."

Rising from her chair, Shana went over and hugged her grandmother.

"Grandma," she said. "I don't think you need to feel guilty about Mom. Somehow I think she would have made a mess of her life no matter what you taught her. She's like that."

"Maybe . . ."

Barbara was out of jail in Paris, Shana knew, but Edith still looked worried.

"Anyway," she went on, "you don't have to worry about me. I'm never going to bomb out like Mom, I promise."

"Your mother isn't a terrible person, Shana. But she hasn't made the most out of her life, either. Somehow I think that you will."

From her grandmother, Shana knew that was high praise.

Later, after taping, Shana and Katie walked up Central Park West toward Katie's apartment. They were going to spend the evening together, learning lines. Shana felt contented in every inch of her body. With things settled between her and Edith, everything was perfect. Well, maybe not quite . . .

"So you'll still be rehearsing at home?" Katie asked after Shana had filled her in on her talk with Edith.

"Yes, but not as much," Shana confirmed. "I'm going to get more time for myself."

"And for Kirk, too, I'll bet," Katie teased.

"Yeah, well . . ."

Shana felt herself blush. Kirk would be back in a couple of weeks for the U.S. Open, and he'd be renting an apartment year round in New York.

The apartment worried Shana a little though. She wondered if it would change his expectations if they had a place to be totally alone together.

"Hey, watch it!" Grabbing her arm, Katie pulled Shana back from an intersection.

"Katie . . ." As they started across the intersection again, Shana turned to her friend to talk about her concern. But she changed her mind when she saw from Katie's tightened jaw and frown that she had her own problems.

She knew what they were too: Mitch, Mitch, and Mitch. Lately his on-the-set temper tantrums had been getting worse.

"Shana?" Katie asked as they started past the imposing American Museum of Natural History. "Do you have any ideas at all about who Mitch's new girlfriend might be?"

"No."

Katie sighed. "I wish I knew. It's tearing me up inside."

"I know. But don't worry. I'm sure things will get better between you two soon."

That was another lie. Shana had a sinking suspicion that things were about to get a lot worse for Katie and Mitch. Some of it might even be her fault. Guiltily, she remembered her interview with Olivia Waxman of *TV Talk* magazine. Nothing had come of that yet, but who could tell?

Suddenly, in typical Nolan fashion, Katie's gloomy mood lifted. Smiling, she held out her arms and did a perfect pirouette. Shana laughed.

"You know what, Shana? I think things *are* going to get better. Did you ever feel that way? Did you even think that just when everything looks the worst, it's *got* to start going right?"

"Katie," she said, laughing. "You're the world's biggest optimist. No, I don't usually feel that way, but I do feel pretty great right now!"

And she did. After weeks of misery, she had just discovered that all around were people who loved her. Katie—Kirk—Edith—

Never again am I going to feel so alone, she thought. If I blow one chance, so what. There's always another. Where people are concerned, the show's never over!

★

ENTER NOW!!! THE "ALL THAT GLITTERS SWEEPSTAKES"
THREE BOOKS!!! THREE CHANCES TO WIN!!!

Win a 3-Day/2-Night GRAND PRIZE TRIP FOR TWO TO NEW YORK CITY . . . INCLUDING HOTEL, TRANSPORTATION, DINNERS.

WIN A FABULOUS EARLY BIRD PRIZE!

If your answer is among the first 500 received with the correct answer to the question found on the entry blank you will win a super "Early Bird" Prize. But even if you are not one of the Early Bird Prize winners, your correct entry will be entered in our Grand Prize Sweepstakes drawing.

SWEEPSTAKES ENDS JANUARY 31st, 1988

NO PURCHASE NECESSARY. Complete this official entry blank or see Official Rules for alternate means of entry.

THIS SWEEPSTAKES CONTINUES IN. . . ."BOOK 3" *FLASHBACK*, ON SALE IN NOVEMBER. IT WILL CONTAIN ANOTHER QUESTION . . . ANOTHER CHANCE TO WIN AN EARLY BIRD PRIZE . . . AND ANOTHER CHANCE AT THE GRAND PRIZE.

1500 "EARLY BIRD" PRIZES (500 for each book). . . .PLUS. . . THREE CHANCES AT THE GRAND PRIZE.

ENTER EARLY AND OFTEN!!! ALL THAT GLITTERS!!! IT'S HOT!!!

ALL THAT GLITTERS SWEEPSTAKES
OFFICIAL ENTRY BLANK

HERE'S YOUR SECOND CHANCE TO WIN. YOU'VE JUST READ, "BOOK 2" *TAKE TWO*.

ANSWER THIS QUESTION:
WHO IS KIRK TUCKER'S DOUBLES PARTNER FOR THE CELEBRITY CHARITY TOURNAMENT AT FOREST HILLS?

_____

_____

MAIL YOUR COMPLETED ENTRY TO: ALL THAT GLITTERS SWEEPSTAKES
P.O. Box 24
New York, N.Y. 10046

NAME _____

ADDRESS _____

CITY _____ STATE _____ ZIP _____

TELEPHONE ( ) _____ AGE _____

OFFICIAL RULES
ALL THAT GLITTERS SWEEPSTAKES

1. No Purchase Necessary to enter or receive a prize. Use this official entry blank or, on a 3″ X 5″ plain piece of paper, hand print your name, complete address, and the correct answer to the question shown on the Official Entry blank. The answer can be found in the contents of *this book* or by sending a self-addressed stamped envelope by December 1, 1987 to: All That Glitters Sweepstakes, P.O. Box 648, Sayreville, NJ 08872. Residents of WA and VT need not include return postage.

2. Enter as often as you wish, but each entry must be mailed in a separate envelope bearing sufficient postage. No mechanically reproduced entries accepted. All entries must be received by January 31, 1988 in order to be eligible.

3. Winners will be selected in a random drawing from all correct answers received by Marden-Kane Inc., an independent judging organization whose decisions are final and binding. Prizes are non-transferable and no substitution is allowed. If the grand prize winner is a minor, he or she must be accompanied by a parent or legal guardian. Taxes are the sole responsibility of the prize winners. Trip must be executed within one year of notification and is subject to availability. Winners may be asked to sign an affidavit of eligibility and release which must be returned within 14 days from notification.

4. GRAND PRIZE (1) A 3-day/2-night trip for two to New York City, including hotel, transportation and dinners. Approximate Retail Value (ARV) $3,500.00. 1500 Early Bird Prizes will be awarded as follows:
Book 1–"Magic Time", (500) A jumbo display digital watch... with day, date, second function and snap close hot pink wide band. (ARV $9.95 each)
Book 2–"Take Two", (500) Your own personalized "All That Glitters" 200-sheet memo pad. Your name clearly imprinted on each sheet. (ARV $9.95 each)
Book 3–"Flashback", (500) An "All That Glitters" all occasion tote bag, complete with web straps for holding on or off-the-shoulder, snap-closure, inside cash and cosmetic compartment. (ARV $9.95 each)

5. Sweepstakes open to residents of the United States and Canada except employees and the immediate families of Bantam Books, their advertising agencies, suppliers, and Marden-Kane Inc. All Federal, State and local laws apply. Void in the Province of Quebec and wherever prohibited or restricted by law. Odds of winning are dependent on the number of correct entries received. All prizes will be awarded. Canadian winners will be required to answer a skill testing question.

6. For a list of major prize winners send a self-addressed, stamped envelope to:
ALL THAT GLITTERS
WINNERS
P.O. Box 714
Sayreville, NJ 08872